Praise for *The Histo*

"Poignant and hilarious . . . Cran‿ ..

between a deceased mother and her daughter as they tell each other's stories to understand each other." —*Los Angeles Times*

"Ultimately, *The History of Great Things* is a story of perception, one well worth reading. It serves as a reminder that what truly matters to each of us is not what actually happens, but how we remember it." —*The Rumpus*

"The novel flows smoothly, and readers game for offbeat narrative approaches will be well rewarded . . . So much like the relationship they're borne of, Crane's deeply realized mother-daughter inventions are therapeutic and ruthless, heartfelt and crushing. A lovely exercise in the wild, soothing wonders of imagination."

—*Booklist* (starred review)

"Co-written, in a sense, by a daughter and her absent mother (who speaks from beyond the grave), this is an important work, fearless in both structure and vision, with Crane's razor-edge fusion of intelligence, humor, and emotion informing every chapter. Get ready, world: this one's going to be huge."

—Jamie Quatro, author of *I Want to Show You More*

"I cannot remember the last time I simultaneously cried and laughed as hard as I did while reading Elizabeth Crane's glorious, tender knockout of a novel, *The History of Great Things*. Wait, yes I can. It was the last time I spoke to my mom about life."

—Amber Tamblyn, author of *I*

"Like everything Elizabeth Crane writes, *The History of Great Things* is wonderful fun to read—smart, insightful, and witty—but it will break your heart, too. It stares down the poignant question so many daughters want to ask: How well did my mother really know me?"

—Pamela Erens, author of *Eleven Hours* and *The Virgins*

"What did I learn after reading *The History of Great Things*? I learned that love survives death. And that no one ever really goes away, even if they have. And that all sides have many stories. And that we make our own happiness. This is unlike any novel I've ever encountered and it's absolutely wonderful."

—Jill Alexander Essbaum, author of *Hausfrau*

"In her signature prose style, full of verve and wit, Elizabeth Crane unpacks the problematic relationship between mother and daughter that will resonate with anyone. By telling each other's stories, the mother and daughter in *The History of Great Things* reinvent each other, their relationship, and the possibility of empathy. You will cry, weep, and be glad you went along for this very particular beautiful and heartbreaking ride."

—Emily Rapp Black, author of *The Still Point of the Turning World*

turf

turf

stories by

Elizabeth Crane

SOFT SKULL PRESS
NEW YORK

TURF

Library of Congress Cataloging-in-Publication Data Is Available.

Cover design by Kelly Winton
Interior design by Domini Dragoone

ISBN 978-1-61902-934-7

Library of Congress Cataloging-in-Publication Data
Names: Crane, Elizabeth, 1961– author.
Title: Turf : stories / Elizabeth Crane.
Description: New York : Soft Skull Press, [2017]
Identifiers: LCCN 2017004910 | ISBN 9781619029347 (softcover)
Subjects: | BISAC: FICTION / Literary.
Classification: LCC PS3603.R38 A6 2017 | DDC 813/.6—dc23
LC record available at https://lccn.loc.gov/2017004910

Soft Skull Press
1140 Broadway, Suite 704
New York, NY 10001
www.softskull.com

Printed in the United States of America
Distributed by Publishers Group West

10 9 8 7 6 5 4 3 2 1

For Ben

Contents

turf

Everywhere, Now

A big black dog sleeps on a sofa in Texas with his paws curled into his chest. The front door opens and a baby person comes into the house with the dog's mom and dad, dog gets up to sniff it, goes back to his place on the sofa. Everything was good right up until this moment; now, uncertainty. And it's raining. Where the rain ends, near the border of New Mexico, a toddler runs into a fuzzy type of cactus, won't stop screaming; her mom can't pull the tiny prickers out, they'll just be there until they're not. In Georgia a little boy wants to enter a pageant with his sister, mom asks him if he wants to be a gay boy, he doesn't know what that means, cries anyway. In Brazil, a five-year-old girl in a dirty dress sees a monkey throw its poop at another monkey, she will laugh about it on and off for the rest of the morning. In London, an expressionless ten-year-old boy in a pristine school uniform leans into the street to hail a taxi, he's got a math test today he wants to do well on, is already thinking about university. At Disney World, a boy gets lost, his dad thinks he's with his mom and vice versa, no one notices for an hour, the kid is crying in front of Snow White's castle. Somewhere in Africa, a kid plays a guitar with a missing string, sings a Michael Jackson song, he's good. If he had a video camera or a computer, it'd be on YouTube, but he doesn't. He's only heard of these things. In Venice Beach, some teenage boys grind their skateboards to a halt beneath an underpass, share a tiny rock of crack, laugh. In Switzerland two teenagers fall in love on a ski trip, the girl will move to the U.S. the next year with her family, this seems tragic at the time, but don't worry, they'll find each other again after a couple marriages and kids. In Daytona Beach, a college girl who lifted her bikini top earlier that day is passed out on a dirty motel bedspread. In a thousand cubicles in a thousand offices, a thousand men are looking at the same blurry online photo of a college girl lifting her bikini top, one of them thinks of his daughter, picks up the phone. Outside, beneath narrow ledges and tucked into alcoves, accountants and secretaries smoke in the rain; they shiver but they never wear scarves. Remember the good old days, when you could smoke in places? In Rome, a woman who won a prestigious art fellowship falls in love with a local, he introduces her to heroin, this detour takes a few years she won't remember much about. Somewhere in the middle of Oklahoma, a UPS guy delivers a package to a farmer who gives him a cup of coffee in a travel mug, says, Just keep it, guy will use that mug for years, think often of that small kindness.

In Seattle, a barista makes a fine latte, looks in the tip jar at three dollars and change, and pushes up a sideways smile as she hands the drink across the counter to a businessman who's applying lip balm with his pinky in a weird way. His lips are very chapped. In Australia, a woman's house just washed away, she watched it from a tree. In Nevada, a croupier didn't take home enough for her electric bill, her cat curls up around her neck, she's got two more days before the lights go off. In India, a man's been at the same desk for ten years, he's good at his job, well liked, but every single day he thinks there's got to be something better, never tries, knows he's lucky, tries to just be happy for a wife at home that makes the dull days worth it. In Idaho, a new wife buys flour with a double coupon, bakes blueberry muffins for her husband. They're a little bit burnt on the bottom, he doesn't mind, they're going to do it again tonight. In Arkansas, a married man believes it's god's will that he sleep with his wife's sister; the sister is not fully convinced, but she's considering it. In Mexico City, a fight breaks out in a bar, a scrawny American tourist takes a punch to the eye but finally breaks it up, feels good about himself. In Chicago, a single woman has a fortieth birthday party, feels the love, her best friend comes from New York, it's one of the best days of her life so far. In Michigan, a woman gives birth to a beautiful, healthy boy; she's disappointed that he has her nappy hair. In Atlanta, a kid gets bullied at school, his mom goes over to talk to the bully's parents, they're surprisingly friendly, apologetic, the bullying continues. Over in Iowa, a lesbian couple, together thirty years, gets married by a justice of the peace, throws a beautiful backyard reception, tiny lights and joy, one of their dads refuses to come. In Philly, two middle-aged brothers take out loans and open a restaurant, it's been their life's dream, but they have no idea what they're doing. In Barcelona a couple is in a custody battle, the husband seems to be winning; privately, but in front of the child, calls the wife an ugly cunt. At a Paris cafe, a guy about to turn fifty realizes for a second where he is in life. He's never been married, never wanted to be, never dated a woman anywhere near his own age, has this moment where he feels lonely for this one second, then buys an espresso for the lovely young lady at the next table. In Nebraska, a mixed-race couple takes in the wife's elderly father; his dementia is setting in to where he often forgets to censor his racist comments, wife expresses shame, husband says, Wasn't exactly a secret. In Montreal, a widow who's been running every day for forty-six years, since she was in high school, blows out a knee, doctor tells her she has to stop running if she wants to keep walking, she has to think about it, takes her time, takes a cooking class, meets an attractive younger man, he's more persuasive than the doctor. On Park Avenue, a seventy-year-old man ends his banking career in disgrace, he's been embezzling from himself since the beginning, his children no longer speak to him, sees that famous baseball player on the news who got booted from the league for doping, had his World Series ring taken back, feels this guy would understand him, tries unsuccessfully to reach out. In Queens, four young actresses share a small two-bedroom apartment. Two of them are from Kansas, best high school friends, the other two they found on Craigslist, they're not from New York either. They're all scared, but only one says so out loud. The other three take the subway into Manhattan for auditions for student films, squeeze each other's hands, they're so excited. Across town in the East Village, a woman who left the city twenty years ago returns with her husband to find things totally the same and totally different. Maybe it's she who's totally the same and totally different, maybe both. It seems to her like the city has been picked up and replaced with a duplicate that still carries all her memories, that even though a lot of it is shinier than it was back in her time, the memories are still, well, less shiny, some of them, a lot of them, even the things that aren't real memories, e.g. people on the street she doesn't know, like some marginally attractive guy in in his thirties but who maybe chain-smoked for a few years with the windows closed, in a black shirt and black pants, sometimes a black hat, smoking, and with a lunky walk—do you know the kind? so many guys have a lunky walk, even the most handsome ones, you don't see a lot of women whose walk is so lunky, there's not much better of a word for it, this long-strided, bouncy, arm-swinging, forward-leaning walk (do you see it now?)—this guy exemplary of a long-ago type that would have taken up some good portion of her time, and what happens when she sees these types, on the street, is that they aren't just passed by, they blur into the real ones, and there is a wish that she could get just a little, just a little of the time back that was spent on these types, because time is moving very quickly now, and just in the one direction, and she knows she wasted good stretches of it on all manner of ill-advised endeavors, and even if she could have let's just say ten percent of her time spent on these types returned to her, she could make very good use of it now. On Fifty-Seventh Street she'll remember that one dinner with a much older man from her office, they used to flirt, should have left it at that, was trying something other than men in black, that direction didn't stick. Over on Bank Street she'll remember that loft apartment she once looked at in Westbeth, wonders if it would have gone differently if she'd moved downtown, if she'd have slipped into a life that made more sense, or if downtown would have just been a variation on a theme. Uptown on Third Avenue she'll remember her first kiss, it was around here somewhere, she's sure, it's a bit of a sweet memory; he was nice, and he's still nice, that's a what-if rabbit hole too. Or where the Palladium was, a dorm now, she'll still think of that one time she went there when it was a club, shared a glance with one of those guys from the Brat Pack, which one was it. On Riverside Drive she'll think of her first therapist, how for years she shook her head to every reasonable suggestion he made, until one day he suggested she should teach, how it was like she'd been pouring nickels into the same slot machine for years and it finally paid out. Down by Wall Street the streets feel haunted, could just be it's nighttime, could be she feels like she's walking on the dust of her friends. Or she'll see some young woman going into Stuyvesant Town who looks like the grade school friend she'd been trying to track down, the one who never turned up on Google because she died before Google was a thing. Or she'll be in a neighborhood that she didn't spend a lot of time in but a restaurant location that's housed nine restaurants since she was last there will bring up dinners she couldn't afford, ones where she drank at home before dinner because drinks were nine dollars, or ordered an appetizer saying she wasn't hungry but it was really because she couldn't afford an entrée, but then the bill was of course always split evenly at the end of the night, at which time she always wanted to yell that she couldn't even afford the appetizer to begin with, remembers when it seemed like a good idea to get a hostess job at that restaurant, but how awful everyone was, the customers and the waiters and the owners, everyone, not approving of her clothes or her shoes or her hair or her ability to do her job (not friendly enough, they said), and that that job, and not a few others like it, usually lasted for a week or two at most. Or a doorway will look familiar, and even if it's a doorway that's been polished up, a doorway that has a nice new security system or some such, she'll remember the photographer upstairs who told her he was also a psychologist and did she mind if he just asked a few personal questions to get to know her better and how creeped out she was but still answered some of the questions before leaving—why? why didn't she just leave?—because don't you know that seven or eight years later that guy was brutally murdered in that very photo studio above that nice security system, by the pissed-off boyfriend of a lingerie model (the term *lingerie* and the lingerie itself and maybe even the term *model* all being used loosely here), and in the photo of the boyfriend/murderer, on the front page of the *Post*, on his way to jail, guess what he's covering his face with, his black shirt. Or she'll see some older guy with a high-pitched laugh at a bus stop who reminds her of the good parts about her stepdad, any or all of it cause for contemplation of her old, less good life, the one where she drank a lot and could not find a boyfriend or a job she ever really liked and was broke always and her mom her mom, with the crazy and the cancer, her mom is still everywhere here, in front of Fairway picking out fruit, on the Lower East Side in front of lighting stores and wholesale shops that haven't existed for decades, in a dishware store in Chelsea Market even though there was no Chelsea Market then and no such thing in that building even, that dishware store was ten blocks up. Sometimes that's not even so bad, some lady on the street carrying an ironing board looks like her mom from far away and she thinks of all the times her mom came over with things she might need, leftover fabric from a dress that could make a cute top, a saucepan, a book about forgiveness (was she asking to be forgiven, or the other way around, still not known, will never be known). You'd think years of therapy would help that some, it surely has, though there she is in her dreams too, again and again, on the days when her specter isn't out walking the street on her behalf. Everything seems different now, the streets have all these rejiggered new weird lanes where as far as I can tell there are parking lanes in the center of big streets like Second Avenue or Columbus. Her husband's never lived here at all, and they're both excited, it is a chance for a bit of a do-over (or for him, just a do) but both kind of scared too, a little bit. Look at where this is going now, so off track, as usual. This was supposed to be universal. Is it even possible for her to imagine a world that she's not at the center of somehow? Let's go back over to Jersey, where a ten-year-old Russian girl arrives at her new home, she's entirely unsure about it. In the UP there's a hoarfrost, sugary coatings of snow on every last needle of every last tree. Everyone's cold there, but they still kind of love it. In Minnesota too. Also in Lapland. In Iceland there's that whole darkness thing, can you imagine? Italian food is so good. Lots and lots and lots of people have cancer, are reading puffy old *Us* magazines with stories of somebody's third breakup ago while they get their chemo. I'd like to go to Spain someday. In Canada there are Mounties. And mountains. There's some bad shit going on in the *-stan* countries, right? What's up with Antarctica, anyway? Am I the only one who gets it mixed up with Greenland? Wait, I think I forgot a continent somewhere, maybe. I was hoping to include all the continents. It's still me, you know that, right? It's always me. Well, here's this: in every town and every city a poem is being written; the percentage of good to bad is unknowable, whether it matters, also uncertain.

The Genius Meetings

On the first Wednesday of the month we meet at one of our homes to discuss our achievements and share our profound and original thoughts. We have done everything from creating mathematical formulas to inventing technologies that will save your lives. We are architects, artists, physicists, and scientists. We are authors, composers, philosophers, and chemists. We are religious men and atheists. We are married, divorced, single, and straight. We know of a gay genius, but he does not attend the meetings. There are no women in our group. We are not saying there are no lady geniuses, but we sure don't know any.

We do not expect you to understand. We always knew we were different. For a minute Frederick thought he was the same, but he wasn't. When he was two, little Frederick sat down at the piano and composed his first sonata, the first to include a solo for the Jew's harp. He thought, Oh, how nice it will be to play this for my little friends! Then his mom came in and seemed surprised, which in turn, surprised Frederick. When Marcus was four he discovered a hitherto unknown genus of insect while his brother was shooting spitballs. When Clifford was six he created a theory of abstraction just the title of which is ten pages long, so we won't bother. Our dear friend William had both crossbred a fig and discovered a dinosaur before the age of seven. These are just a few of the sorts of stories we share when we meet.

We meet to congratulate ourselves but also to purge ourselves. We meet to share things we cannot share with you. Smart things but also customs. Like the metaphorical value of sleeping in a nightcap, to keep the genius in. Or the fact that many of us hold on to what we collectively refer to as our "lucky things" (ranging from common items like the shirts or socks we had on when we won awards, to typewriters that don't work, to small locks of hair purportedly from the heads of geniuses that went before us), though not one of us believes luck has anything to do with it. Or the value of saving entire volumes of academic journals, every article ever read that pertains remotely to our work, nay, every scrap of paper we ever touched, just in case, even if it means we must delicately navigate around the towers of paper in our homes and offices. Or the need for exactitude and precision, the importance of a regimen, and the malignment and misunderstanding of anal-retentiveness in contemporary society. We are aware that there are those of the mind that our disciplined ways of life are harsh, that our strict routines have consequences both mental and physical; to this we say, maybe so, but you sure seem to like that electricity we got you. We meet to have a safe place to use words like *ateleology* and *apotheosis* without confusing or embarrassing anyone, and away from your judgments of pretension. We meet to smoke pipes filled with tobacco we brought back from foreign lands and drink one brandy or liqueur that lasts us the evening. We meet to talk about that time Eldred, a philosopher, smoked marijuana, and to thank him for sparing us that horror. We meet to talk about one painting by Schiele or one article on Hindemith for two hours. We meet to discuss papers that do not get published and tenures that get passed over. (These things don't happen often, but when they do, the despair is often paralyzing.) We meet to talk about theories that don't pan out (or are disproven! the worst!) and novels that remain imperfect and therefore unseen and possibly published after our deaths (edited so thoroughly wrongheadedly as to diminish our genius when redemption is no longer possible) and discoveries made by those not among us, and the years lost on these projects. We meet to talk about how hard it is to be a genius. We discuss the difficulties of never being wrong, and the loneliness of being the smartest person in the room. We talk about the ones who died too soon, of the great works of art or science not to be. We grieve for Hubert, who took his life at the mere age of thirty-four while composing an opera that was sure to become a masterwork (a devastating loss to Frederick in particular, as Hubert had become a mentor of sorts). We weep for the great doctor Thirlby, who leapt to his death in the throes of a manic episode before finishing that remedy for autism. We talk about our personal lives, the lone area in which we do not always excel. We often suffer from depression and even mental illness. We make poor choices. We marry only the most beautiful women, models and movie stars. One of us has married both a Miss America and a Miss Universe. Some of them are quite bright, some less so. There is nary a genius among them. That is not what we want. We geniuses love a gorgeous woman with a problem.

Take Winston the rocket scientist. Recently Winston came to the group with a broken heart. His wife, Amaravati, a Bollywood star, left him for one of her costars. I should have known, Winston told us. I know everything else. We all nodded, knowingly. We asked if there were any signs. Well, he said, perhaps when she told me that she could not promise to be faithful, I should have listened. Otherwise I can't think of anything. We nodded again. How could you know? we asked.

Or take the time Eldred, who has suffered from often crippling depression since graduating college at age ten, came to ask the group whether or not it might be time for him to go off his medication. He posed to us the idea that since he had been doing quite well for several years on his lithium, there seemed to be no reason to stay on it. The group had some differing opinions on this. Some of us fully agreed that this was a reasonable argument. Others were less sure, suggesting that a medical doctor would know best. Eldred ultimately made the decision to go off his meds with results that may have involved imaginary kittens with police badges providing dangerous directives, but we are happy to say he is now back on his meds and doing much better, although his choices in women still fit our general profile. His most recent fiancée was a woman he met in the psych ward. Theirs was a passionate but stormy affair, although this one actually lasted longer than most of his relationships.

And the renowned architect Phillip has been living with his partner, the violet-eyed supermodel Elsabetta, for three years, trying unsuccessfully to cure her of her sexual abuse issues. It has been his belief that his sexual prowess and willingness to try anything to please would relieve her of these issues, but he has so far not met with success, and cannot figure out why. We stared at him blankly. We have nothing, we told him.

Or take Geoffrey, the child of two academics, whose story resembles that of many a genius we have known. The pressure for young Geoffrey to achieve was immense, beginning as soon as he could hold up his head on his own. Geoffrey's parents taught him sign language when he was only two months old and began labeling the entire household inventory with large flash cards so that Geoffrey would learn to read before his first birthday. Passing that milestone at ten months, his parents began to read aloud to him from Tolstoy, Dickens, and

Hemingway, and Geoffrey was subsequently enrolled in everything from fencing to ballet class to tennis lessons. Tutors were brought in to teach him biophysics, dead languages, and medieval history. He learned to play the harp like a seraph. For fun, they would do the crossword, or play chess. Geoffrey never saw a checker until he was thirty-one years old. He grew up to teach macroeconomics at Yale, but his secret shame never left him, and it was one nearly all of us shared. Geoffrey, in grade school, had once gotten a B. In penmanship.

Geoffrey hung his head when he told us this, but we had all been there. In fact, on this night, we took turns sharing our poor grades and the humiliation and fear they brought upon us. We recalled the harsh talk of permanent records and less than perfect GPAs* from our parents and principals and deans, and our long, carefully considered pleas to our professors to reconsider for the sake of our futures. We were aware that there were many who considered a B-plus to be a respectable grade, but this merely widened the gap between ourselves and everyone else. How could we live with a partner who believed such a thing? How would we raise our children? Would we go the other way, and try to love them simply for who they were, as we had longed to be at tender ages, as we often long to be now? Or would we do as our parents did, pushing our children toward the heights, at the risk of again handing our conditions down? Sandor the botanist pointed out that in the real world,

* 5.0 GPAs became popular after our time, for which some of us give thanks to god.

no one mentions these things, that when the prizes are handed out, our A-minuses and B-pluses have long been forgotten by everyone but ourselves. And yet these are the things that shape us and haunt us.

The story of William is perhaps less typical but ultimately most illustrative of our common plight. William was the only child born to a family of Nebraska fig farmers. His father was a stoic man, not given to open displays of affection, but dedicated to creating the perfect, juicy fig. His mother, who had hoped for a large family, five or six siblings for William at least, would suffer three miscarriages before sickly William was born. Worse, though, was the loss of their firstborn, Alma, who died of unknown causes in the night, just before her second birthday. William would never know this sister, only that he wasn't her.

William discovered his particular genius as a small boy. Like many boys, he was interested in dinosaurs, and could name all the classes, subclasses, and infraclasses by the time he was four. By age five, having exhausted the meager selection of literature on the subject at the local library, he begged his parents to buy him a book he'd seen in the card catalog that wasn't on the shelves. His father dismissed this pursuit of dead things as irrelevant, but told him if he worked on the fig farm, he could save up his money and buy whatever books he cared to. William eagerly accepted this challenge and unintentionally smited his father by crossbreeding what turned out to be the perfect fig (sweeter, plumper, and moister than any before it and readily identifiable by a tiny fragrant bloom on the bottom end), for which he was silently scorned. Nevertheless, he bought himself a shelf of dinosaur books and by age six, theorized that there was a dinosaur that had not yet been discovered. By age seven he'd appeared on *Merv Griffin*, *David Susskind*, and *60 Minutes*, and by the time he was nine, bones of an unknown dinosaur species were unearthed in Peru, confirming his theory, at which time William was honored by the Field Museum. His father made him work on the farm until he was fifteen.

He didn't have time to be awkward in high school, since he emancipated himself and graduated the year he turned fifteen, but he more than made up for that at college. One time, William drank three light beers and became wildly intoxicated (we relish these tales of debauchery, as we cannot afford to be heavy drinkers; as much as we might like to cease our brain activity for an occasional evening, we cannot risk the long-term damage), almost threw up, and slept until nine the following morning, earning him the nickname William the Lightweight for the duration of his time at university. Subsequent to this, William dated a number of emotionally withholding women, which he found to be an exhilarating challenge. After discovering yet another unknown dinosaur the summer after his sophomore year, he met his first wife at a sorority mixer. William was of course not in a fraternity, nevertheless his roommate, who had taken pity on him, invited him to this party, where he met Coreen, who, quite drunk on wine spritzers, thought William was funny and agreed to marry him. William, later noticing that she preferred wine spritzers to his company, divorced her shortly thereafter. This, however, did not deter him from marrying two more alcoholics, a professional cheerleader and an especially stunning barista. He simply cannot stop getting married. William has been with his current wife, Marla (dean of a small arts college), for nearly five years (his longest by four and a half and considerably longer than most of the rest of us, with the exception of Frederick, whose thirty-year marriage to Louisa, a renowned sommelier, is an extremely rare example of endurance, one we all admire and fear with equal fervor), and the problem seems to be, as far as we can tell, that Marla is basically normal, and smart, and wants to talk and work on their problems. William and Marla have one child, a four-year-old girl, and William would like to have another, but the couple's constant disagreements about parenting are a major concern. Marla wants to send their daughter to a Montessori school.

Whoa, said Clifford. That is so not cool.

We all nodded at the great truth of this.

Also, she's very into this idea of "play" for children, said William.

Confused looks rippled around the room like the wave at a football stadium.

Marla doesn't think Zooey should have extracurricular activities until she's at least six and/or only if she expresses the original interest herself.

Well what does she do all day? asked Marcus.

Exactly, said William. I don't know. She just plays.

Oh man, said Geoffrey.

Plus Marla thinks it's fine for her to pick out her own clothes now.

Oh, that is no good, said Winston.

Really? said William. See, I just don't know sometimes. Do you know what I wore every single day until I was fifteen?

We did know, but William told us again anyway.

Overalls. Overalls and a red-checked shirt. Like a character from *Hee Haw*. I wore that outfit on *60 Minutes*, even.

Hearing this again didn't lessen the impact. We did feel his pain.

I mean, so my kid wears polka dots and stripes once in a while, at least she's expressing herself.

Mmm, I don't know about that, said Clifford.

Yeah, that's iffy, said Phillip.

Okay, but why? William asked.

It just is, Phillip said.

Everyone nodded, but no one had a better answer.

I don't think you can let this continue, Geoffrey said. Manipulate her, was his idea.

Yes! Marcus said. Also, tell her one thing, but do another.

Mess with her mind, Phillip said. Tell her she's brilliant on Monday, and on Tuesday tell her she's obtuse.

Ooh, good one, Clifford said. I'd also advise backhanded compliments.

Are we talking about my child or my wife? William asked.

There was a brief silence.

Your wife! Eldred finally said. Another silence. Right?

Yes, wife, sure, definitely, we said, with uncertain nods.

Do not let her dress or feed the child, Winston said. Or go to work. Or see her friends. We couldn't argue with that. Well, Clifford tried to suggest it might be all right for her to have friends, but the rest of us shot it down.

Where do you think they get these crazy polka-dot ideas? Winston added.

William reminded the group that we were geniuses, not misogynists.

No, some said. We're both.

This got us sidetracked for a while.

Dump her ass, Eldred said. She sounds like dullsville. We all vocally agreed.

William told us that Marla suggested marriage counseling, and that he was really considering it.

Hmm, we all said. Not what we'd have done.

Let's take a vote! Phillip said. Raise your hand if you think William should break it off.

The vote was, of course, unanimous. William left the group

disheartened but determined to break it off until he arrived home to Marla, who had baked him a pear tart and presented it to him wearing only an apron. Seeing his lovely bride holding the tart, William's heart softened, and he immediately agreed to go to counseling.

At the next meeting, William reported of his success in marriage counseling. He tried to explain about the tart and the apron. We understood the temptation. We have seen Marla. He told us of insights and revelations he experienced in their counseling sessions. That Marla actually had things to teach him. That compensation for his childhood feelings of inadequacy with a series of beautiful women had left him unfulfilled. He explained that when people do not have conflict in a relationship, it is considered a success. He used terms we were familiar with but which baffled us in this context. He spoke of open-mindedness, communication, trust, and honesty. He spoke of serenity and spiritual awakenings. We mostly stared at him blankly as he made these reports. Sensing his imminent departure from the group, we snapped out of it and tried some last-ditch efforts to persuade him to end things with Marla. We suspected rightly that he was sharing our secrets. She's going to get old, we told him. And ugly, we said. Hideously ugly. Also fat. Very fat. They all get fat, eventually. Bald, probably even. Oh, definitely bald. We knew we were grasping at straws, that William was already gone. We were wildly jealous, but we kept that to ourselves.

We still take in new members every so many years, when we hear of a new genius. Now and again at the meetings William's name will come up. Wonder how that William is doing. We know, of course, that he's still married to Marla and that they have another toddler who is apparently only in preschool. Imagine how fat Marla must be now, we say. So fat. And bald. But some of us have seen photos of Marla, who has to be near thirty-four by now, and she is neither fat nor bald. We speculate that William's genius has diminished, but we know it is untrue. What no one wants to say is that we envy him. We secretly imagine our lives with one perfect woman who will take us away from ourselves, spirit us away on clouds and whales and the shoulders of giants, who will show us things we have never seen, and with whom we will stay forever.

We meet to discuss whether to donate sperm. On this we are divided, even in our individual minds. Some of us believe the world could use a few more geniuses; others do not want to see more suffer as we do. We talk about how thinking physically hurts sometimes. How we wish we were dumb. How we look at the blissfully dumb people and we imagine what that's like, you who never think of killing yourselves just to have one quiet moment. We pity you, but we envy you. We think we are better than you and worse than you. We wish you could understand. Be grateful that you can't.

Star Babies

First the star babies took over the state of California. Star babies multiplied rapidly in Los Angeles, slowly pushing out all the other babies, out into the Valley and as far east as Joshua Tree. Star babies took over Palm Springs and San Diego, although they were stopped before they could enter Tijuana. They had no identification. Those star babies turned back and headed north. Star babies took over Barstow, Bakersfield, Fresno, Sacramento; star babies entered San Luis Obispo, Monterey, and Big Sur. Star babies liked surfing. Star babies knew the way to San Jose, San Francisco, and Oakland; star babies sat in on classes at Berkeley; star babies drank up some wine at Napa. Star babies made camp in the redwoods, made claim on Lake Tahoe, and then pushed into Nevada. Star babies won big in Las Vegas. Las Vegas was putty in their baby hands. In Utah, star babies converted Latter-Day Saints into sinners. Star babies landed in Eureka, but they didn't stop there.

Some states were easy. Most of the western United States was pretty easy for the star babies. They were laid-back in Oregon and Washington, sparsely populated in Idaho, Montana, and Wyoming. They were compliant in Arizona, Colorado, and New Mexico. The Dakotas were easily taken, Nebraska and Kansas weren't looking, and Oklahoma didn't see them coming either. Star babies knew better than to go into Texas unprepared, so they took Arkansas and Louisiana first. Star babies were bigger than Texas. Star baby factions spread across Louisiana and into Mississippi, Alabama, Georgia, and Florida. Star babies dominated in the South. Star babies hit it big in Nashville and moved into Graceland. They settled in Kentucky and the Carolinas. Star babies went into the central states, winning Missouri, Iowa, and Nebraska in a single day. Minnesota and Wisconsin went quietly after that. Star babies took their time in Illinois and had their way with Michigan. Indiana went without a fight, as did Ohio. Pennsylvania was resistant, briefly, but relented.

Star babies moved quickly through those little states on the East Coast, and the nation's capital was almost too easy. In the nation's capital star babies actually gave them a head start. In New York they were feisty, but they liked it, and eventually star babies had their way. The rest of tri-state area did not put up a fuss. Massachusetts required a smallish effort, but with the support of Kennedy babies, they couldn't lose. Star babies almost forgot about Rhode Island, but were reminded by Vermont and New Hampshire, who were bitter about the loss. Star babies lived in historic New England homes and ate lobster in Maine.

Star babies did not forget Alaska and Hawaii. Star babies left Puerto Rico alone.

Everyone in the country was a star baby. Everyone knew who every baby was, what every baby was doing at all times. Everyone knew what every baby wore, what every baby ate, who every baby slept with. Paparazzi babies were confused for a while, because they were star babies too. Do we take pictures of ourselves? they wanted to know. Of course we do, they told themselves. Eventually, the paparazzi babies had paparazzi too.

Star babies were charming, rude, and clever. They were cunning, baffling, and powerful. They were bright and dull, deep and shallow. Star babies were spoiled brats and great humanitarians. All star babies were beautiful. Some star babies were descendants of other nations: England, Nigeria, India, Spain, China, Japan, Finland, Hungary, Brazil; some star babies were of Russian descent. Some were from outer space. If you looked at their DNA, you would always see a high percentage of star baby, because star babies stuck to their own kind so often as to create new strands. Some were known for what they did, but all were known for who they were, or who their ancestors were.

Star babies had names like Bling (common, like Jane or Brittany), Jester, Anubis, Alabar, Absence of Malice, Ruffle, Pleat, Pocket, Whip-Stitch, Doily, Gob (also common), Funnel,

One-Pipe, Quodlibet, Chaiselounge, Ottoman, Vampire Bat, Babe the Pig, Piglet, Planet, Powder, Seersucker, Orliza Doolittle, Dachsund, Deathwatch Beetle, Cloverleaf, Cheat-bread, Toaster Pastry, Quail Egg, Egg Substitute, Executive, Executive Branch, Mortadella, Perpetuity, The Cloisters, Close the Door, Cheeky Monkey, Mango Chutney, Dragonfly, Funny Boy, Munificence, Mushroom Cloud, Iron Man, Go Speed Racer, Go Dog Go, You Go Girl, Esther Rolle, Rococo, Fleur de Lis, Flexor, Houghmagandy, Pilcrow, Panorama, Pig in Wellies, Metallica, Pox, Phlox, Bok Choy, Trussell, Tufthunter, Tomato, Wassail, Fuji Apple, Fig, Rhubarb, Wolfberry, Beetwater, Booyah!, Day-Glo, Seat of the Pants, Groovy Is as Groovy Does, Picnic Basket, Resort Wear, Revelation, Think Again, Abandoned Luncheonette, Sound Magazine, Miami 2017 and Scenes from an Italian Restaurant (brother and sister), J. D. Salinger Esq, Grace Paley by Comparison, Cat's Cradle, Archie Comic, Phosphorescence, Komodo Dragon, Lute, Mummy, Mumblety-Peg, Lapis Lazuli, Lake Michigan, Light-Emitting Diode, Lightning Bug, Light Opera, Simoleon, Smithy, Sturm und Drang, Stardust, Stardom, Starlet, Star of Bethlehem, Star Chamber, Stargazer, Starfish, Starlight, Starflower, Star Spangle, Stargate, Starmageddon, Star Master Flash, Star-Nosed Mole, Starry, Starburst Flavor Blast and Stars and Stripes (star names were very popular for obvious reasons), Nouveau Monde, Novelty, Magic Wand, Beekeeper, Birkin Bag, Linsey-Woolsey, Lapsang-Souchong, Chai, Cookie Dough,

Jane's Crazy Mixed-Up Salt, Elizabeth Wurtzel XIII, and President Barack Obama (very common as early as 2009). Star babies wanted their children to have completely unique names, but they forgot about the collective unconscious. Case in point, three Frosted Toaster Pastries were born in separate cities on the very same day in 2014. What a story that was!

Star babies reproduced for several generations until a small number of them began to have questions. They said, What's so great about being a star baby anyway? Maybe we'd like to know something else.

There's nothing else to know, the star baby majority said.

The star baby minority set about finding out.

It was a small minority.

At first it was just a few star babies, a couple or three dozen up in Maine who dared to share their increasing discomfort in a world where everything and everyone was known, where everything and everyone was perfect. Admittedly, it was hard not to like being beautiful and rich and sleeping on mink sheets. No one could argue that they minded mink sheets, but these few star babies simply wanted to know what else there was. Plenty of star babies offered to tell them what life was like before. People went around without chefs! star babies said. Without trainers or bodyguards! Or personal doctors! they said in hushed tones. We have heard that they kept things to themselves! star babies said. Some say that as many as two people slept in the same wing of the house, still others told the curious star babies, shaking their heads at the thought of it. Urban legend, they said.

So some star babies were confused. In some ways these things didn't sound so bad to them, but in other ways they did. Not only did they not know how to cook, many of them didn't know the word *cook*. Few star babies had known life without an adult nanny. Still, some star babies longed to keep things to themselves, and thought it would be a delight to share a wing with someone, maybe even a single room, whispering secrets and sharing toaster pastries, the food. When they were young, these star babies had read *Little House on the Prairie*, long understood to be a horror story, imagining only how lovely it might be to live in a tiny cottage with little sisters to teach things to and loving mothers and fathers right there beside them. These star babies got D-pluses from their personal teachers on *Little House* book reports, who accused them of misreading the book entirely and gave them pluses only because of their perfect penmanship and spelling.

After much consideration, some star babies set out on their own to become unknown. Inexperienced, they failed to pack well. In camouflage Louis Vuitton cases they brought with them cashmere throws and ermine pillows, they brought golf clubs, rock candy, vacuum cleaners, and cartons of milk, televisions, million-dollar bills, dinner jackets, dinnerware and dinner theater, birdhouses and spas, wedding gowns and wind chimes, armchairs and armoires, floaties, flags, fireworks and Ferris wheels, hams and hammocks, sourballs and solariums,

Sub-Zeros and subwoofers, subdivisions and submarines; they brought estate jewels, bathtubs, bonsais and bon mots, elevator music and élan, hippapotami and howler monkeys; they brought puppies, popes, and presidents, Paris in the '50s and pickled beets, clowns and Clydesdales, vaults and valentines, Tinkertoys and tambourines, showgirls, shamans, gargoyles, game theories, and gamma rays; they brought Harvard and Yale; they brought the Chrysler Building, the Brooklyn Bridge, and the Guggenheim, the Washington Monument, the Bean, the Space Needle, the Statue of Liberty, the Gateway Arch and Disneyland; they brought the Santa Monica Pier, Navy Pier, and Pier 1. They brought golden notebooks and diamond pens, lamps instead of flashlights, encyclopedias instead of maps. They brought platform boots instead of hiking boots. They brought toasters and Picassos, PlayStations and pepper mills. They brought banned books like *Moby-Dick*, *The Odyssey*, and *The Phantom Tollbooth*. They brought the darkness before dawn, the dawn of the new age, and Dawn dishwashing liquid. They brought menorahs, metronomes, and marionettes, seashells, sea monkeys, and sea change. They brought robots, racing forms, and red herrings. They brought these things because they didn't know they couldn't. Anything they brought that they actually needed was purely by chance.

The curious star babies had intended to time their escape to coincide with just one star baby media circus, but as good luck would have it, not one but three star baby stories exploded on the same night: the birth of tween pop sensation Booyah!AP-44-08-96's[*] first child, the latest sightings of rumored canine lover Funny Boy HK-26-89-71, both cavorting and canoodling with various Afghan Hounds, and the high-speed police pursuit of accused star baby murderer Metallica SP 32-72-92, who had endeavored to flee the country in his personal airplane. Any one of these events might have been enough to tie up most of the paparazzi babies, all three was a godsend.

The curious star babies headed directly for the woods. Most star babies were not into camping. Star babies walked as far as they could and spent their first night at the base of a fir tree. Star babies found that they enjoyed the sound of the birds and the sight of the stars and the cool breeze and they wondered aloud what the big deal was until they remembered about weather, which they remembered only when it began to rain, heavily. Star babies wished that even one of them had brought a raincoat instead of a bookshelf. I thought about it, said one. But look at these great books. Curious star babies nodded in agreement. What about the Guggenheim? Couldn't we sleep in the Guggenheim? Or the Chrysler?

It was pointed out that all the buildings and monuments were quickly abandoned due to their excessive weight.

All of them? they asked. Even the colleges?

---

* In these times, because names were extensively hyphenated, and although their birth certificates list their entire last names, babies with more than four hyphens were given a number, something like a social security number, but not, because that doesn't exist anymore because all star babies are very, very wealthy.

Also gone, said others.

It was too bad about the colleges, some of them might have put those to good use.

Surely we held on to the Statue of Liberty, said one.

It was bogging us down, said another.

What about the Bean?

Gone, they said.

Dammit. I loved that shiny Bean.

I know, it was shiny, right?

So shiny, they agreed, eyes down.

The next morning the sun appeared and the green things smelled greener and the star babies were not dead due to being unseen, as they had been warned was a possibility.

We're alive! they said.

It's a miracle! they said.

Oh, calm down, others said.

Star babies had spiritual awakenings almost as soon as they reached the perimeter of the woods. They took in the fresh air in giant gulps. They felt cool and warm breezes on their skin. Star babies were accustomed to complete climate control, being allowed outside only if the temperature was between sixty-eight and seventy-two degrees. They happened upon purple blooms poking out of cracks in the ground, sunlight landing on pine needles, baby deer drinking from sparkling streams, and found themselves mesmerized to the point of transcendence, with sudden and profound understandings of the entirety of nature, with sudden and profound understandings of their (small but wondrous) places in it. Each experienced this in their own way, but none less profound.

Look at this fantastic woodland creature! Who but a benevolent god could have created such a life! I have never seen such a thing! one said, kneeling down before it in prayer.

That is a mushroom, said another.

Whatever it is named, I shall heed its power from here out.

Good luck with that, said one more, who had recently turned his will over to a snail.

Several, who had seen water only in plastic bottles, immersed themselves in the icy streams, pledging their allegiance to the divine flow. Others dunked themselves facedown against their reflections in placid lakes, believing that their own images were the faces of god before them.

No, David Foster Wallace and Gromit, that's you, said the Riverites and the Mushroomians.

Still confused, they explained further. It's like a mirror.

How do I know this mirror does not show me the god of my understanding? That god does not appear exactly as I do, but lives flatly in the lake? DFW&G inquired.

The Riverites and the Mushroomians could not answer this. The Current-Day Owlets suggested they agree to disagree. That they should carry on with their intended purpose, to find the anonymity they sought and believe as they so chose.

By and large, these experiences were genuine; the star babies had received the big, if unexpected, payout for their quest. All they had wanted was to be unknown, and what they had come to know was beyond their simple dream. They simply shook the apple tree, and the universe delivered mushrooms and snails. Others, however, tried to force it, attempting salvation via tree frogs, who eluded their grasp, or praying to bees, who stung them.

Soon, some of these star babies began to turn back. One refused to give up his PS166.

But we have no electricity anyway, they told him.

Some infighting began at this time. There had always been concern about discovery, but with some of them dropping out, there was greater fear than before.

Death to turncoats! some star babies said.

That is not very spiritual, more peaceful star babies said.

There was some violence.

Eventually, there were just a few star babies left in the woods, and though they were clever, and remained a step ahead, they could feel the presence of star baby paparazzi closing in. Star babies took residence in the trees, building a small village of two-room houses out of wood, mud, leaves, toasters, and other random materials they had brought. (In addition to a single handsaw, others had actually brought hammers and nails.) They wallpapered their tiny homes with million-dollar bills (having no use for currency), they made their Picassos into tables with peppermill legs, they made beds out of wedding dresses stuffed with the hair from their heads, and they played checkers with snails and acorn caps. They sang songs about their new lives and had tree dances and ate berries and fish and built swings from vines and baseball mitts, and they called themselves family. Star babies had unknown babies. Just plain babies. It was quite lovely for a time.

Unfortunately, turncoats wasted no time telling all upon their return to the known life. It was just their way, all they knew to do. Looking back, they couldn't have kept it to themselves if they'd wanted to. Even the returning star babies who didn't speak about it openly were followed by more photographers than ever before, who hoped to capture on film some iconic image, some residue of the unknown life. Mostly, though, the stories they told captured the imagination of a nation, and suddenly everyone began heading for the forest, hoping to get a glimpse of the unknown life.

Things went downhill from there. Or should we say downtree.

Star babies headed for the forest in ridiculous numbers, with them the paparazzi and all the media. Many of them too had spiritual experiences upon the discovery of nature, but almost as many were frightened by bunnies and quickly headed back for the safety of their castles.

The pioneering star babies were right back where they started, kind of. At least to the extent that the photographs of them in their cashmere sarongs and ermine booties were on the internet within moments of being taken and their tree homes appeared in *Architectural Digest*. They were unwitting and unwilling style makers. Star babies had their stylists fashion outfits out of whatever was in front of them, record-cover dresses and picture-frame earrings; restaurants began serving Fresh Fish on a Plate (unscaled, just the fish); and star babies had their mansions moved up into the trees.

Needless to say, the woodland star babies were up in arms about it. Though they liked to think of themselves as an inclusive people, their tree villages became overcrowded and the obscurity they so desperately sought was once again a thing of the past.

If there was one positive to all this, some small but enterprising bands of star babies around the country fled the cities in search of genuine anonymity and endeavored to begin quiet, spiritual lives of their own, in deserts and on mountains and plains, at beaches, lakes, and even abandoned mini-malls, anywhere they thought they might go unnoticed. Word of this phenomenon quickly spread.

Star babies had woods, plains, and mini-mall meetings, politely but futilely asking photographers and news media to kindly respect their privacy.

Star babies talked among themselves and brought up the subject of war.

No one wanted that. They had one final plan.

Star babies protested, marching with signs and paper bags on their heads. Star babies lay down on the ground with paper bags on their heads. Star babies held candlelight vigils and circled their trees with paper bags on their heads.

Paparazzi babies ripped off the paper bags and some set fire to them without even bothering to remove them from heads.

So, war.

There was no doubt that it would be hand-to-hand. The star babies of the United States, having everything they thought they could possibly want and having agreed at NISBATO (No International Star Baby Treaty Organization) never to occupy foreign lands, had become neutral long ago, and had abolished and destroyed all weaponry. Except nuclear. Just in case. They, of course, kept this from the rest of the world, and it obviously wasn't an option in terms of protecting themselves from themselves. They really hadn't imagined it would come up. Life had been too perfect, they thought. And so when the war came to pass, the star babies were unprepared. They tried to send their star baby entourages, but their entourages had entourages, who had entourages, who had entourages, and eventually these entourages all came back around and met at the beginning. Really, if you think about it, both sides were equal, except for the woodland star babies had thought about it and strategized creatively with their limited resources, and the rest of the star babies, not really.

So the woodland star babies kicked and punched and smashed cameras and poked eyes out with sticks and diamond pens. They whomped people on the heads with chandeliers and flat-screens, trounced them with armies of hippos and Clydesdales, just plain frightened them away with howler monkeys. They threw rock candy and rock lobster. They camouflaged soldiers in whatever they had (the furs and the nine-hundred-dollar camouflage pants came in handy here) and sent them to the deserts, lakes, and mountains to communicate and ally with other growing factions. They exploited nature and weather in any way they could. In the mountains of Vermont and New Hampshire they bunkered in snow caves and hurled ice balls; in the fog they crept along the ground and stabbed their enemies in the ankles with broken champagne flutes and broken lightbulbs, clobbering them on the heads with wind chimes once they were down. In the deserts of New Mexico and Nevada they made catapults out of dead trees, lobbing cacti and rocks. At the oceans they slapped them with fish and octopi and defeated their enemies easily because anyone who wasn't hit was totally grossed out. At the American shores of each of the Great Lakes, they used trickery, promising spiritual salvation in the reflections of the waters and drowning them with their bare hands. Similar promises were made at the Grand Canyon, Niagara Falls, and the Hoover Dam, where unwitting star babies were brought to the edges in hopes of seeing god and instead were hurled over the edges, smashing their skulls on the rocks or impaling themselves on branches. In the Everglades, Mushroomites proclaiming themselves to be Alligatorians walked their foes into the mouths of waiting predators who swallowed them in single bites.

Star babies of the cities were close to declaring defeat when an emergency summit was called at which the last-resort subject of nuclear arms was raised.

What other choice do we have? suggested generals and kings.

Give them what they want? asked advisors and knaves.

Never! they said. They are trying to take away our right to photograph as we please, they countered.

No one had a counterpoint to this.

Moves were made quickly, buttons were pushed, and epic explosions took place.

Errors occurred. Big ones.

Everything was flattened, mountains and buildings, forests and cities. Star babies were flattened as well.

Meaning they all died.

Except for three star babies who had bunkered down in a sewer. They emerged confused, and smelly. There were no woodland star babies among them.

They explored.

They found rubble. They found no more star babies, no woodland creatures, no mushrooms.

They took each other's photographs.

Look at this! said one, showing a photo of the second to the third.

He doesn't look so good, said the third to the first.

Let me see that, said the second, grabbing the camera and hastily snapping the other two. Look. You guys don't look much better.

That's because it's a bad photo.

You took it too fast, said the second.

Let's take a selfie!

Star babies bunched together and smiled for the camera. The first held it as far away as he could to get the shot.

None of us look very good, they agreed.

Let's try another one.

The second wasn't very good either.

The third was a little better, but the second star baby didn't like the way his hair looked.

The fourth was better for the second, but the first star baby had his eyes closed.

The fifth was better for the first and the third, but the top of the second star baby's head was cut off.

Several dozen poses later, they still hadn't gotten one good picture.

I'm hungry, said one.

Me too, said another.

Let's go get something to eat.

I don't think there is anything to eat.

The first took a picture of the third, hungry.

Wow, look how hungry you look, said the second.

You look hungry too, said the third, snapping his photo.

Let's take a picture of us all hungry, said the first.

The group agreed that they all looked very hungry. They contemplated this for a while. Then they photographed themselves in contemplation of their hunger photo.

This is really harshing my mellow, said the second.

This is you with your mellow harshed, said the first.

The second looked at the photo and nodded. That is harsh, he said. I had no idea. Thank you for showing me that.

I'm starting to forget the last time I even had a mellow, said the third.

This rock looks pretty good to me, said the first, taking a lick of it.

Let me try that, said the second, grabbing the rock.

The third took a photo of the first and second fighting over the rock.

Get a hold of yourselves! Look at you guys, he said, showing them the picture.

We're fighting over a rock, they said.

We're not going to make it, said the first.

The second took his photo.

This is you realizing we're not going to make it, he said.

Yeah, well, you're not going to make it either, said the second, showing the evidence to the first.

None of us are going to make it, said the third.

A photo, then.

Roosters

I am pretty sure a bag of kettle corn or two is just what I need. I'll just get three. Because today I am going to be kind to myself. That is what the books say I should do and so that is what I will do. I will start by treating myself to whatever I want. Here I come, fancy cheese. I am sure that the most expensive cheese in the store is exactly what I need. I am pretty sure that if I pair this cheese with this olive bread, this will be the ticket. I bet some figs will go well with this too, and some honey. I will need a few bottles of this blackberry grape drink too. Also cookies.

But what if it's these bath puffs that would make me feel better? These bath puffs are on special for a dollar. I bet this whole Jacuzzi-sized bin of bath puffs would be just what I need. But this Longhorn section interests me too. If I started collecting Longhorn stuff, orange shot glasses and orange travel mugs, orange foam horns, orange pens and orange plush football rope toys, I would feel full of heart. If only I felt less indifferent to Longhorns, or if I were from Texas, or into football, or any kind of sports, or if their team color were a deep midnight blue, or if there were a Ryan Gosling section, if I could get a Ryan Gosling trucker hat or Snuggie or baby bib, then surely, things might work out for me.

There is a jewelry store within the store now, I see, and I could imagine that jewels might make me feel a way that I'd prefer, but these don't really appeal to me. It seems like they don't appeal to anyone. There is no one at the grocery store jewelry store, which saddens me for the jewelry store man, and though I could go and clean out his jewelry store, because I have given myself that permission today, sadness is to be avoided. Probably if I swept down this whole aisle of vitamins, just cleared the shelf off right into my cart, that would work, that the mere promise of vitality contained within the bottles would restore my good cheer. Or if I went down the office supply aisle. I love office supplies. Office supplies always make me feel better. Or what if I bought all the gift cards in the store, a thousand of them, and sent them to all of my Facebook friends? Giving always makes me feel a good way. Or what if I went and ordered a cake the size of my living room? That would surely be great. A giant cake and all the flowers in the flower section. And balloons. All the balloons. And all the patio furniture, plus all these giant metal roosters. Actually they might not have enough metal roosters here, I see only about twenty, and some of them are small. I'd have to order more roosters from other stores. Because I'll bet, if I could set up these roosters, got enough to cover the whole front yard, nothing unwanted would ever get in.

Here Everything's Better

The Tall Woman

1. On one side of the store as you walk in, there's a clothing section, mostly orange, Longhorn stuff. This section also has large bins with random specials, bath puffs, ten-dollar holiday gift sets, things like this. I usually pass this section by, but today they have some plaid cotton sundresses I look at for a few minutes.

2. In the drugstore section, there are dozens of brands of shampoo on one side of the aisle, varying in price from about six dollars up to fifty, no lie. The Suave and the VO5 are across the aisle on two smaller, lower shelves. My thoughts:
    (a) if you're looking at these, you shouldn't be looking at those, and vice versa.
    (b) the bottles on the expensive side are a little smug in their numbers, a little too certain that everything is better on their side.

3. In the bulk section, I see a beautiful woman shoveling out some flax. This woman is taller than my husband, who is six foot three. When I get home and tell him about it, he says he's seen her there too, in the bulk section. That's random, I say. Well, I tend to notice when I see a woman taller than me, he says.

What Sweet Is

1. The following week I'm in the bulk section again but they're out of blueberry granola. I sigh, loudly I guess, because as I move over to the raspberry granola, I hear someone say, Sorry about that, I took the last of it, and turn around to see the tall woman, reclining on the bottom shelf behind me, eating a bowl of it. She's got a whole setup, like bunk beds: a thin little mattress and blanket on the bottom, with a clip lamp above her head, some books, plants, and a few dishes on the shelf above her, clothes on the next shelf up. I turn back to finish scooping my granola, figure I'm just seeing things.
2. A few days after this, my husband comes home and tells me he saw the tall woman at the grocery store again. I ask him if she was sleeping in the bulk aisle. He says, No, but that's so weird, she was in there reading a magazine. What magazine was it, I ask. What *magazine*? he asks.
3. The next time we go to the store together, my husband tries to show me how to pick out fruit again. You have to look for apples that don't have bruises, he says. Okay, but how do I

know if they're sweet or not? This kind is sweet, he says, pointing to the Fuji. That isn't true, I say. You don't know what sweet is, he says. No, *you* don't know what sweet is, I say.

The Dress Again

1. On my way into the store, in the Longhorn section, the tall woman is looking at the plaid sundress. She sees me trying not to look at her, says, This would look better on you. You think so? I say as she hands it over. I do, she says. You should get it. Thanks! I say. Something about this has really brightened my day. I pick out some nail polish to match.
2. At home, I model the dress for my husband. I can tell by the way his eyebrows are wiggling that he wants to sex me. I know what sweet is, he says.
3. After, I wash my hair with the Suave, rosemary mint. It smells nice, lathers up good. Stupid snobby shampoo aisle, I think.

I Try Not to Take Things Personally

1. I wear the dress to the store the next time I go. Frankly, this is the only thing I've worn since I got it, besides pajamas. My husband has sexed me every day.
2. The tall bulk-aisle woman is in her bed reading a book this time, a well-worn copy of *Underworld*. Oh, I just finished that book! I say. She smiles politely, though it seems genuine.

I'm momentarily embarrassed about my enthusiasm. She notices my dress. Was I right or was I right? she asks. I'm suddenly moved to invite her over for coffee. No thanks, she says. I try not to take this personally, because I can see her contentment with her place on the shelf. She doesn't need anyone else's coffee.

3. At home I ask my husband if he can imagine living at the HEB. Um, no? Aren't you the one who's always saying we should pare things down, live more simply? I ask. I meant like in a yurt, he says.

It's Me from the Store

1. Walking the dog one afternoon, I see the tall woman walking down my street. Oh hey, I say. She doesn't seem to recognize me, so I say, It's me. From the store. Which, as soon as I say it, seems like the weirdest possible thing I could have said. She waves but keeps walking.

2. I just saw the tall woman walking down our street, I tell my husband when I get home. He doesn't have any real response to this. And? he finally says. That's all, I say. But don't you think that's weird? Now it's weird that she's *not* in the store? he asks.

3. She's not at the store the next few times either of us go (when my husband goes without me, I always ask), and most of her things are gone too. There's a toothbrush on the middle

shelf, and there's a boy sitting on the bottom shelf looking at an oldish *People* magazine that I'm pretty sure was hers. I'm about to tell him he probably shouldn't sit there, that that magazine doesn't belong to him, but his mother calls him before I get the chance.

The Bagels Suck

1. Well, I was never really a huge fan of this store anyway. It's one of those super giant ones. You can't just run in for one thing, and if you're almost done, down at one end of the store, and you remember one more thing you needed down at the other end, if you're like me, chances are you'll just go without it. The bagels suck. It's the closest store to our house, but it's not even that close. We're moving away soon anyway.
2. I bring up the "Where do you think we'll live next conversation" again. I can't seem to help myself, though I know my husband will just remind me, again, that we've got another year and a half here at least. That I should try being in the moment. But I need to mentally prepare, I tell him. I don't like this moment. Yeah, me neither, he says. This moment *sucks*.
3. Here's a thing I really love about my husband: When I feel a loss, even if it's some small thing that I know he probably thinks is weird, he always sits with me until I stop crying.

This Moment Also Sucks

1. We live in upstate New York now, where the grocery stores are normal sized, but you have to go to three different ones to get everything you want. No one lives in any of them, as far as I can tell, and there are no good bagels here either.
2. All that said, I prefer these inconveniences. A grocery store shouldn't be the size of an airport. It's too much. If there's room for residents to go unnoticed in the bulk aisle, there's too much room. The store closest to me, I almost never go to unless I'm out of something super basic like butter or eggs or bread. It's one of those generic stores that's never guaranteed to have the same things the next time you go back. Still, when I'm there, the product names never fail to amuse me. I once bought a box of cereal called Circus Balls and a bag of Bold Old Salty Sticks. Also this store sells pregnancy tests at the checkout line, which always makes me wonder who only remembers they need this when they see it by the register.
3. This moment also sucks, but in a different way than it did in Texas, and I don't think the next moment will be better. I can hang with this moment. The landscape suits me here. And I'm tired of moving, though the nature of our work makes it inevitable. But what if we find a town with the perfect grocery store, my husband will sometimes say, which, I won't lie, gives me pause. But I almost always answer, We live here now.

Some Concerns

I am afraid that this shirt does not go with this sweater. I am afraid that my outfit does not match. I am afraid that my outfit is too matchy-matchy. I am afraid that because I like orange, you will think I am a Longhorn, but I am also afraid, in Texas, that you will not like me if I am not a Longhorn. I am afraid to conform, and afraid to stand out. I am afraid of being a fashion don't. I am afraid that I do not have what the magazines say I should have: a classic white shirt, a trench coat, and a little black dress. I am afraid that I dress too much like a student.

When it rains, I am afraid that my bangs will become totally fucked up, and that you will think that I styled my hair this way on purpose. I am afraid that you think I mean for my roots to show, when in fact I have an appointment for color next week.

I am afraid of the undertow. I am afraid of water moccasins. That sounds like it might be a nice thing, a soft slipper to wear wading into a pond, but it isn't. It's a snake. I am afraid of snakes. I am afraid to dream about snakes. I am sometimes afraid that my bad dreams about snakes will come true. I am sometimes afraid that my good dreams about anything will not.

I am afraid of doing the wrong thing. I am afraid of not knowing what the wrong thing is. I am afraid that I think I am supposed to be at the faculty meeting, but that I am not. I am afraid I may have missed the deadline. I am afraid that the paperwork I am filling out is incomplete, and that it will not be processed. I am afraid that I should have enrolled in the ORP, even though I am not certain what the ORP is. I am afraid that I am doing something that is against the law, but that I do not know the law. I am afraid that I do not have all the information. I am afraid it may be too late, and that I have already done the wrong thing, many times, and not known it. I am afraid that I have the odd-even lawn-watering thing wrong, and that I will water my lawn on an even day when I should have watered on an odd. I am afraid of getting in trouble, even though I am no longer in third grade. I am afraid of embarrassing myself. I am afraid of saying the wrong thing. I am afraid that I have been calling you Lizzie when your name is Leslie. I am afraid of gaffes, faux pas, and mistakes. I am afraid that if I say the wrong thing, you will never forget it. I am afraid that if I say the wrong thing, I will never forget it.

I am afraid I have forgotten something.

I am afraid of leaving things out overnight. I am afraid that this orange I am eating, which was left out overnight, might be bad. I always smell the milk before I drink it, just in case.

I am afraid to drive my husband to the airport. I am afraid that if I don't drive my husband to the airport, I am a bad wife. I am afraid of many things as relates to driving. I fear left turns. I fear that at a left turn with an arrow, I will move to the head of the queue when there is no arrow, when there is only a green, which means you have a chance to go, but which is essentially the same as no arrow. I fear driving west anytime between 4:30 and 8 p.m. (depending on the time zone) when the sun is at a level that renders the blinds useless. I fear blind spots. I fear trucks. I fear high, curving overpasses. I fear any road high enough to be described as *breathtaking.* I fear that the common meaning of *breathtaking* is perhaps not what I am looking for in a driving situation. I fear streets with no names. I fear crushing squirrels, and I fear crashing into a pole to avoid them. I once crushed a possum, and the sound was something no one should know.

I fear that I will miss the bus. I am very fearful of being late. I do not know what I think will happen if I am late, but I do not want to find out.

I fear crossing in between.

I am fearful, living near the expressway, of what we are breathing. I fear, living in a very old house, that it might burn to the ground. I am afraid, if all of my things burn in a fire, that I will lose my memories. I have already lost more than enough memories.

I have some concern that I do not eat well enough. I fear that popcorn, even with Parmesan cheese on top, is not a nutritious dinner. I fear that I don't get enough exercise, although I am not fearful enough to start exercising.

I am fearful of sleeping alone in a house. I am fearful that I will forget to lock both doors, or that I will lock the door but that my keys will still be in the door. I have done this, and when my neighbor rang my doorbell at 2 a.m. to tell me so, I was frightened. I am fearful that locks don't matter anyway, that criminals will pick the locks, or break the windows. I am fearful that the dog will need to go out at 3 a.m. and that there will be criminals hiding in the yard. I am fearful that if there are criminals hiding in the yard and I need to call the police, my cell phone will be dead. I am fearful that sleeping alone in a house, I will not sleep. I am fearful of sleeping pills. I am fearful that in a crime, I would lose my ability to scream.

I have been fearful that I might commit suicide, accidentally. That I might, entirely unrelated to my state of mind, jump out of a window.

I have some concerns that this dessert I am eating was doused with pear brandy, and that I will get drunk.

I am afraid to sing in public. I am afraid that I am a fantastic singer who wasted her talent. I am afraid that I think I am a fantastic singer, but that I am merely able to carry a tune. I am afraid that if I sing in public, you will know me.

I am afraid of being found out. I am afraid that if you look me in the eye, you will find me out. I am afraid that if you look me in the eye you will find out things that I do not know myself. I am afraid that I am unqualified to do anything I might get paid for. I am afraid that I am not smart enough or well-read enough. I am afraid that I will say stupid things at academic parties; that a conversation about *Ulysses* will begin, and that I will not have read it, and that someone will suspect that I have not read it, due to my unconvincing nodding, and they'll refer to the part where Ulysses eats a tamale, and I will continue my nodding and they will say, Aha! I am afraid that my students like me, but only as a person. I am afraid that I will not get everything done. I am afraid that I will die before I get everything done, and that no one will finish it for me, or they will finish it wrong.

I am afraid of things my dog might do. I am afraid that I am a bad dog parent. I am afraid that my dog will swim out too far and get caught in the undertow, or that he will run into the road, or get lost, and that if he gets lost, he will be so afraid not knowing where he is or why I'm not there. I am afraid that my dog will get out of the fenced-in yard. I am afraid that my dog will fall out of the car. I am afraid that my dog will get into a fight with another dog and that I won't be able to stop it. I am afraid that my dog will get into a fight with another dog and that I will try to stop it, but that will result in injury. I am afraid that my dog will one day catch a squirrel or a bird, and that he might catch a disease. I am also afraid that if he catches a squirrel or a bird, I will have to clean up the mess. I am afraid that my primary concerns about the result of my dog catching a squirrel or a bird not being the death or suffering of the squirrel or the bird makes me a terrible person.

I am afraid that when we disagree about our dog-parenting styles, my husband will leave me. I am afraid that when we disagree about anything, my husband will leave me. I am afraid that when we have been married for forty years and we disagree about anything, I will still be afraid that he will leave me. I am afraid that one day I will be old and my husband will leave me. I am afraid of menopause. I am afraid that when I go through menopause, I will grow a huge lumberjack beard, and that I will become cranky. I am afraid that I am in menopause now. I am afraid of the number fifty, as it relates to how old I am. I am afraid that one day I will be old and infirm and my husband will be burdened by me, and not say so. I am afraid of cosmetic surgery. I am afraid of Botox, and so should you be, but I am also afraid of wrinkles. I am afraid that my husband will die before I do, but I am more afraid that I will die before him. I am afraid that if I die before he does, my husband will find a terrible new wife. I am afraid that this terrible new wife will throw away my sweaters, eat off my dishes, and think that she is my dog's mommy. I am afraid that this terrible wife will think that she understands my husband, but she will not. I am afraid that the terrible wife will nod when my husband talks about art but will be thinking about her next manicure. I am afraid that the terrible wife will be everything that I am not, but not in a good way. I am afraid that the terrible wife will have an annoying accent, and that she will decorate my home with "paintings" and bedspreads from the hotel outlet. I am afraid that the terrible wife will shop at Costco, and that my garage will fill up with industrial-size tubs of Combos and ten-packs of Speed Stick. I am afraid that my husband will have hot sex with the terrible wife, but that he will be quietly lonely. I am afraid that the terrible wife will seem like a fantastic wife, but that she is really a trickster. I am afraid that I am a terrible wife.

I am afraid that when my husband becomes a famous artist, we will have to move to New York. I am afraid of moving back to New York. I am afraid that I will not just be a small fish in a big pond, that I will be a small fish afraid to leave her apartment. I am afraid that in New York, I will only leave the apartment to walk the dog, and that I will be wearing pajamas and giant slippers. I am afraid that New York is different than it was when I was growing up, but not in a good way, and not enough to erase my past. I am afraid that if I move back to New York, everything good that happened after I left there will reverse.

I am afraid that I am a bad daughter. I am afraid that I am a bad sister. I am probably an okay aunt.

I am afraid of change, and I am afraid of staying the same.

I am afraid that we will run out of oil. I am afraid that when we run out of oil, and can't go anywhere, that my farming skills will be insufficient. I am afraid that when I kill the crops on our farm, we will slowly starve to death. I am afraid that when we run out of oil, we will also run out of electricity, and that there will be no TV. I am afraid that if there is no TV, there will be silence, and that I will have to pay attention to my thoughts.

I am afraid that my thoughts are not normal.

Where Time Goes

Antarctica. There's just a ton of it there.

Unused web addresses. Looking at you, jonpshea.net, .tv, .biz, .everything. It's a common misconception that it goes to actually looking at the internet. But it's actually in the internet itself, and it isn't easy to get out, thanks to people like this.

Tote bags are never really empty, even when they are. Granted they don't hold much. But if you have a couple dozen sitting around in your attic, you might find an hour or two in there.

For sure some is with the socks that get lost in the dryer, let's just put that out there right now. Some also gets in between couch cushions, but that time gets mixed in with all the crumbs and dust and doesn't amount to much. You can vacuum up that time and not feel bad about it. Grout is porous, so a lot of it slips out that way. But this isn't about how it goes, it's about where.

The Kardashians have tons of it. It can actually be bought. Most people don't know that. People go by the saying, but sayings don't know. Here are some other wrong sayings: *time flies, there's a time and a place for everything, time reveals secrets, all in due time, a stitch in time saves nine.* I could break down each of these for you, but you're smart, you can figure it out. *Time heals all wounds* is the most boneheaded though. And there is totally time like the present. We'll get to that later.

M____ is hoarding a lot of it. I don't want to name her though because she's working through some of her issues.

J____ also has a stockpile but his prices are bullshit. This is the thing. If you want to buy it, it costs a shit ton of money. But that said, you can get it for less than this.

A____ has a warehouse full of knock-off time. Trust me, this is not what you want. It's no different than a Grucci purse. One use and it starts to fall apart.

S____ has a vast supply and will give it away to anyone who plans to make good use of it. But S____ has some weird ideas about what good use means. She has watched no fewer than eighty YouTube tutorials on how to create a perfect eyebrow. She'll give it to you if you say you want to start a puppy mill. Partly that's because she doesn't listen. Especially if something like *puppy* is in the sentence, the rest falls away.

Q____ has a great deal to spare and will happily donate to anyone for anything anytime as long as it doesn't hurt anyone, no judgment. Just maybe don't tell her everything, because she's a gossip.

B____ has three extra months. Currently, she's squandering it. That may not be totally fair, but that's what it seems like to her mom, who's dead. Time is different when you're dead. We'll come back to that.

There are any number of houses that are harboring extra, but in most cases, these areas are inaccessible without dismantling walls or ceilings. Chimneys invariably have time in there, but even most of the sweeps don't know this, and it usually gets cleaned out with the soot and that's the end of that. Likewise with smokestacks.

There's a two-family house in the Bronx where there used to be a lot of it in the basement. This was one of those basements with a number of different rooms, some finished, some not, a laundry area, a half-bath, an extra refrigerator, a deep freezer, not so surprising, a lounge area with a scratchy old plaid sofa bed, a black-and-white TV on a rickety metal cart, and one of those ancient exercise machines with the belt where all you had to do was stand there with the belt around your hips and let it shake you (you always had high hopes for this, when you were eleven and wore Chubbette-brand hand-me-downs from your cousin, but all that machine ever did was make your butt itch), then you step down out of this lounge area into the room where the boiler is, also nothing unusual, then you step down again into another long skinny room where there's a storage area, some of your childhood stuff got put there in the '80s (you're not sure anymore what all besides some artwork and maybe a cigar box of seashells), a breakfront holding a collection of ceramic poodles, silver-plated candlesticks, a few odd vases with dusty plastic flowers stuck in, a candy dish with Jordan almonds wrapped in tulle from four different weddings in the seventies, also boxes and boxes from the grandparents and their grandparents, some of that came with them on the boat from Italy, loose photos of unsmiling people in dark coats, handwritten names on the back like Ugo and Paola, a crocheted infant bib, a crumbling linen baptism gown, a cracked patent leather purse (contents: crumpled hanky, Max Factor compact, a corno with a broken tip, Loew's Paradise ticket stub), a ratty fox-fur collar (head and feet, yes), then there's another room behind that, more of a skinny hallway, not room to store anything, and then there's a door at the end of that room/hallway that you were told goes outside, but that isn't true. It goes to time, and this particular time is exactly like the present. But the door to this time was left locked, and the new owners of course tried to open it, broke the lock, only to find a cinderblock wall, which they could have easily figured out by going outside to where the door would open out to and seeing—yeah, cinder blocks. But there's actually several inches between the door and the cinderblock wall and the walls of the house, and a ton of time is just floating around in there. This is just one of the ones we know of, but the point is, if you look for it, it might turn up in places you wouldn't have much reason to think about. A lot of this time was left behind by the former owners of this house, all of whom eventually died there. These people did the best they could with their time, but they didn't know the truth about how much was getting out via that door. The true story is that when the house was built, the basement was intended to be a rental unit, and that some years later, after that never came to pass and someone broke in (in fact, through an upstairs window), their best idea to prevent further break-ins was to get a German shepherd and seal up that door. But the story that got handed down was a tale that changed depending on who told it to whom; sometimes it was extremely tall, where if you were a grandchild or a visiting niece, it might involve sea creatures or ghosts. Your favorite version was the one your stepdad's father told you, about how there was another world behind that door, one that was the exact reverse of the world you were in, another basement identical to this one, only the other way, filled with all the same things, and upstairs, all the same families eating all the same meals, pasta, calamari, capicolo, brasiole, having the same fights, imbecile!, pazzo!, Big Enz yelling at Little Enz (forty-nine years old now, Little Enz forever), smoking the same cigarettes, another German shepherd, the whole thing. Nothing at all different? you'd ask; Nothing except for everything, he would always say. And you'd try to picture it, some version of you over there, a version of you that was more clever, or bold, or wore brand-new clothes in non-chubby sizes, or didn't care what size your clothes were, like that girl Nancy in your homeroom who would say, Jealous? to whatever fat-horrible derision that got thrown at her, or who just had a wardrobe of the coolest sneakers on the planet to make up the difference between how much you cared and how much you wished you didn't, or who caught the eye of your stepcousin's friend from camp across the table, the one you never saw again, not knowing he thought about you for the rest of that school year while you wrote entire plays about him in your diary, even though the totality of your conversation was two barely audible *His*, not knowing that that version of you was picturing the same thing, or would have, if it were true. We can't say if it is or isn't, but it seems true.

We don't suggest waiting until you're dead to find it. That might seem to go without saying, but that saying *better off dead* didn't entirely come from nowhere, sarcasm of the sentiment aside. It's just that when you're dead, the reality is, you've got all of it and none of it. You get that, right? What's not to get? Nothing you do while you're dead exists in the same kind of time. It feels like there's more of it, but that's a false illusion, plus, that turns out to provide zero satisfaction. Don't confuse what we're describing with hell; granted it might sound hellish, but all it is is just something different. Hell and heaven are ideas for someone else to get into. We don't know whether or not they exist; we personally don't think they do, but we're only experts on time. And when you die, time is kind of like this: you have all the time to do whatever you want, but what you quickly learn is that it's more or less without meaning. You can literally read all the books when you're dead if you want to, but that knowledge goes nowhere, and worse, you won't feel anything about it. It's just like, Oh, that's a book. That's ten books. That's a hundred books. Look at me, I read a thousand books. Except not really. There's no payoff. You don't even get the satisfaction of bragging. It's like a diet of all candy. It's the first thing everyone does when they die, but the ensuing conversations are literally endless, and, sorry for the pun, deadly dull. You finally have time to take up sewing, you take up sewing, you might end up sewing for a hundred years, very relaxing, you lose track of time, end up with enough clothes to wardrobe the world's poor people for generations, but you can't get them into regular time, because you're in dead time. Anything you wanted to do in regular time you can do to your heart's content after you die, but it's the heart's content part of it that's taken out of the equation. You can do whatever you want to your heart's absence after you die.

So the point is, death isn't a viable option, if it's time you're looking for. There is one other place where it goes, though as far as we know it's an unreachable destination. It's in the horizon. Seems obvious, right? Try to get to the horizon sometime though. People have. It's a popular idea that you can get there by boat. From which the best you might bring home is a spectacular photograph and a nice memory. You're not going to retrieve time from there because the horizon you see isn't the actual horizon. I mean, that's obvious, we have to call it something, but a little-known fact is that the horizon is an actual location. I don't want to get into tears in the universe or whatever here because that seems a little more sci-fi than what it really is. It's more like: Picture something like a cube. A transparent cube. But which can be filled beyond the obvious capacity of the cube. A sizeless cube. It doesn't have to expand or contract. It's just the size that it needs to be. Into it goes: All lost moments. That brutal fight you had with your sister, all the screaming hot ninety-seven minutes of it. Every single time your boyfriend called you a name, every single time you forgave your boyfriend for calling you a name. So many drinks after the one that got you that sweet buzz. So many. So many cigarettes after the one you smoked with your buddy from down the block when you were ten that made you throw up. (I know. That one after that thing that one time, that one was good. I kind of want to give you that one, but that one came after nine thousand packs, so I just can't. I'm sorry.) So many lies, big and small, when you really blew it, missed your baby's first giggles right in the other room because you were starting that email affair, when you missed your kid's fourth-grade violin concerto because you were trying to break it off. So many lies when you didn't want to do something, when the truth would have been easier and might have brought you toward someone instead of away. So many thoughts about why you ever smoked another cigarette after your first one made you throw up. So many thoughts. Thoughts both oversized and undersized, any thoughts not the exact size relative to the accomplishment. Thoughts related to curing cancer and holding the hand of a cancer patient are allowed equal time, any overages go here. (Sorry geniuses.) Thoughts related to writing a prize-winning novel versus telling a good campfire story, both overages and underages go here. Great storytellers don't always give themselves their due, if they work in some nonliterary field, though prize-winners often give themselves more. That guy who just brings a guitar to the barbecue, plays the Beatles songs while everyone sings along? The baby who was crying all afternoon until everyone sang "Blackbird" wants everyone involved to give themselves their due, but no more. All thoughts related to what you did wrong, after the first one. Even if you did something wrong. All thoughts related to what you did right, after the first one. Yep. Silences go here as well, not the good kind, the kind when something, anything should have been said. Another myth exploded: What happens in Vegas goes here. Along with a calculated percentage of your video game time over and above your productivity and time spent with friends. The cube has a whole series of math equations for time use, each one designed for each individual. There are allowances for so-called trivial things. Anyway, all the terrible things go in here, things you wish you'd done differently, but what also goes in here is color. Color goes in here, color that if you could see it, would make you think you hadn't really ever known what color even was before; think of the amber color of your dog's eyes when the sunlight hits them just so, and the good feeling that gives you, and then imagine that every color is represented in this way, and all at once; that might seem like too much to think about but in reality, together with a warm wind, and the scent of all the flowers, and music, kind of a lulling percussion, a pleasing hum, it's transcendent. Together with your losses, these things make time into something more than time, something better. For now, the only way to access it is to imagine it.

I know. We're telling you where all this time is and you say, well, you can't afford a ticket to Antarctica, or you don't know any of those people who have it, you can't get to the horizon, or whatever. You have three kids, you have two jobs, you have no job, you're taking care of your dad who calls up to you from downstairs four times every night in a panic about his balled-up tissue that fell to the floor. He's worried that the cat will eat it. I know. I am going to give you some of mine. I'm going to give you five minutes right before you go to bed every night, just for you. Promise you'll keep it.

Looking

I like looking at pictures of Gwen Stefani. I do not need to know any more about Gwen Stefani than that she looks really good in red lipstick. Looking at pictures of Gwen Stefani in red lipstick with pale skin and pale hair and a white tank top and a baby on her hip provides as much information as I feel I need about Gwen Stefani in order to imagine Gwen Stefani in the way that I want to imagine her. Very occasionally, I like listening to Gwen Stefani, but listening to Gwen Stefani does not affect the way I look at Gwen Stefani and what I get out of looking at Gwen Stefani. When I look at Gwen Stefani in her red lipstick I think maybe I should try red lipstick one more time, just to be sure, though really, I know the truth, and my red-lipstick desires are almost fully satisfied by looking at pictures of Gwen Stefani. All that said, had Gwen Stefani never come into my line of sight, the likelihood is high that I would not feel that anything was missing.

I like looking at photographs of New York City in the 1960s and '70s to see if they remind me of something I forgot. I like looking at old advertisements. I like looking at B movies on Spanish-language channels. I like looking at some of your pictures on Facebook, even when I don't know you. I like looking at your bookshelves. I like looking at everything in hardware stores and stationery stores. I like looking at my grandmother's sewing machines when I go out to the garage; they look like snazzy old cars, though they each weigh about forty pounds, I don't know if they work, and I only ever look at them when I'm looking for something else. I like looking at tall shoes that cost a thousand dollars. I like looking at two men kissing. I like the slightly electronic thwacking sounds of the automated postal machine, which I suspect could have been made to be silent but were made to have this sound so that the user might feel a sense of accomplishment, a certainty of delivery, and which could have been any sound, a bell, or a chime, but which was decided, finally, to be a thwack. I like the sound of *Car Talk* in the background on Saturday mornings more than I have a regular need for the content of the program. I like seeing old maps on your wall. I like seeing old black men wearing hats so much. I like seeing bodegas, though I rarely go in. I like looking at sculptures by Jeff Koons. I like looking at street art, sometimes, like when they cover lampposts and things with sweaters. I like looking at craft websites. I like to look at my craft supplies; I like to look at your craft supplies and see how they're organized so much more interestingly and efficiently than my craft supplies. I like to look at numbers. I like looking at the same old brownstones again and again and again. I like looking at old warehouses with broken windows surrounded by vacant lots filled with weeds and rabbits. I like looking at Girls Gone Wild commercials in the middle of the night when I can't sleep, the ones on network TV with the body parts blurred out. I like looking at videos of awkward twelve-year-old boys lip-synching and dogs and puppies and cats and kittens and anteaters and anteater babies and unlikely animal friends.

Some of these things I would like in my house, some not, although mostly that's beside the point. At first I thought I should simply say I look at these things, instead of I like to look at these things, but because I look at them for as long as I do, or as often as I do, I have decided that I must like looking at them, otherwise why wouldn't I look away? I dislike looking at as many things or more, women in dresses with only one sleeve, new subdivisions with no trees, anything I'm told is intended to be "shocking," grisly things in movies, the trash that blew onto your lawn, and the big gray sky. I dislike the word *ugly*, the sound, the meaning, the implication, though it is occasionally useful in instances of describing a blackness of heart. There may or may not be rhyme or reason to any of it. Sometimes I try to wish these things away that I do not like and there they still are.

All the Wigs of the World

Bigwigs are everywhere, all around us. If you are the biggest wig in one world, you can be sure there is another world with a bigger wig than you. If you are not the biggest wig in your world, there is still a good likelihood that there is a smaller wig than you. If you are sure, though, that you are the smallest wig in your world, do know, that in other comparable worlds, there are still smaller wigs. And what about this: What if there's a whole other world where everyone wants to be the *smallest* wig? Think about *that* for a minute. There are always bigger wigs and smaller wigs. There can be no biggest wig or smallest wig. Think about it: Who would decide such a thing? A panel of wigs? And even if a fair panel of judges was agreed upon by all the wigs of the world, how then, to measure big and small? Height? Weight? Dollars? Rupees? There are too many ways to go, too many variables. Best to just try to find a wig that fits well. That right there is no small thing.

Mr. and Mrs. P Are Married

Mrs. P is born on a cold day in West Virginia in 1947, eyes open, to a homemaker and a general practitioner. Worrying everyone terribly, she does not speak until her third birthday, when she says, I have to go. No one knows what this means. When directed toward the bathroom, she looks in and shakes her head. The child is immediately signed up for Catholic school.

Mr. P is born in Los Angeles, California, in 1941 with a slap to the bottom that literally knocks the shit out of him, and it's not so much a sign of what's to come, it's the opposite if anything, as it is the first in a long series of unfortunate incidents.

His parents had once been in vaudeville, if that has anything to do with anything. We doubt it, but just putting it out there.

Upon turning thirteen, Mrs. P's mother cuts her daughter's long blond hair into a Jackie-style bob, which does not suit her. It's the latest thing, her mother says, but Mrs. P will have short hair only one more time in her life, which will also be a mistake. Mrs. P loves her mother (if not as much this day as others), but she is now and will always be a daddy's girl. (I'm hideous!/Baby girl, you couldn't be hideous if you grew a camel's hump on your back. Hair grows, sweet thing, you just hold on./She hates me, why else would she do this?/Sweet pea, your mama doesn't hate you, I reckon she's just a speck jealous because the bloom is off her rose and yours is just opening up.) Mrs. P wonders for a moment what will happen when the bloom falls off her own rose, but as soon as that thought passes, she tears off for the dime store, where she pockets a mascara and a "Fatal Apple" red lipstick. In addition to bloom-loss prevention, young Mrs. P hopes this will bring some edge to her style, and this look isn't really her either, but she gives it a good go for the better part of seventh grade. However, this move does not bring her great popularity, and she quickly remodels herself one more time with a ponytail and a smile. This will carry her a long way.

Mr. P, tall, skinny, and Irishly handsome, gets into some trouble the summer before his freshman year of high school, the usual 1956 fare: smoking behind the bleachers, fistfight on Sunset Boulevard having something to do with a girl, drinking/throwing up whiskey into Echo Park Lake. His punishments escalate accordingly from grounding for a day to a yardstick-whipping, and these whippings will continue throughout his high school career. From this Mr. P will learn two things. Thing one: that yardstick-whippings modify his behavior only for the length of time it takes for the physical pain to go away (a lesson Mr. P the elder will not ever learn). Thing two: just because yardstick-whippings as a method of parenting may not be effective does not mean he won't keep it in mind. (In fact, when he has his own children of yardstick-whipping age, he will not resort to this, but he will consider it, often.) Mr. P is not the dumbest guy on the planet, but he's not super quick.

Mrs. P joins the pep squad in high school and is nominated for captain before the end of the year. She has become quite a natural beauty, although in the brains department she's pretty much on the level of her future husband, maybe a half notch up. Mrs. P does spend a lot of time thinking, about life mostly, she just doesn't get very far with it. She looks at the world around her, and it sort of looks nice, post-football bonfires, pie-baking contests, Main Street parades, church potlucks, but even from the center, she feels removed from it somehow. It looks to her like a class photo they took without her. She thinks she's supposed to want it, but imagines everyone walking around with nothing but clouds in their skulls because it's easier than coming up with any idea of what they really think. At times she wishes she had clouds in her own skull in place of thoughts like these, but even the effort to assimilate only results in further thoughts about why no one sees what she sees. She tries to enter the picture by dating the quarterback, Ned Crawford, for most of her junior and senior years of high school, leaving him devastated when she decides to break up with him right before prom. Ned had been planning a prom night proposal, but Mrs. P had been secretly fucking her mechanic since he fixed her Ford Falcon. The mechanic had seduced her, quite easily, with talk of life's small beauties: the Baptist church on South Elm just after it lets out, the Potters' old blue barn that leans like a parallelogram, a pink Band-Aid on a boy's skinned knee, the percussion of a car engine. He talks at length about the details that give meaning to the mundane. (It's not about looking, it's about seeing, you dig?) Mrs. P has never heard talk like this before, certainly not at home, and Ned speaks mostly of football and taking over the family shoe store, neither of which interest her. The mechanic sparks more in her than her sexual nature (which is no small portion of her overall nature); it's almost as though he activated a hidden mechanism or replaced a missing part she'd hardly known was gone, and suddenly she feels as though her whole self has finally been assembled. When she tells him she needs to go, he nods and sends her off with a farewell fuck. After reading a tiny ad for an art school in the back of *Photoplay*, Mrs. P takes off for Los Angeles, just before graduation. Disheartened to discover that the art school is actually just a suburban post office box, she redirects and answers a casting call for all-American types for a game show hostess in the same magazine. She does not get that job, but lands a mayonnaise commercial right after putting in an application at the Chicken A-Go-Go.

Mr. P is at this time on the amateur boxing circuit, mostly getting his ass kicked, but it doesn't matter, because a talent scout from one of the networks spots him and offers him a screen test for a new soap opera. Mr. P, like Mrs. P, had shown little interest in acting before jumping in (in spite of occasional suggestions from his parents to try bringing back vaudeville) and his talent hasn't quite been uncovered at this point (although he does have some), but on the basis of his resemblance to the actor hired to play his brother, he's given the part. The show becomes a hit and Mr. P makes the cover of *Photoplay* and Mrs. P sees it and thinks he's kind of cute in a bland sort of way, a guy who manages a grocery store kind of way, but she won't give him another thought for fifteen years. At this time, nineteen-year-old Mrs. P is involved with a much older television producer who gets her a few lines on some popular situation comedies and not much more. She's not with him for this reason, that's not her thing, and she's not with him just because he tells her she has a quality (because she has no idea what this means), nor is she with him because he talks to her as though she understands what he's talking about (even when she doesn't). She's with him because when they fuck, he does this thing with a scarf around her neck that makes her feel like Jesus himself is fucking her.

Mr. P at this time, has not gotten much further, sexually speaking, than pounding his costar missionary-style. This is good enough for making a baby, which they do, a red-headed girl they call Maggie, but not good enough to hold on to his costar, who briefly becomes his wife after they discover the pregnancy. They divorce quickly, because his drinking has sent him on one too many two-day benders, and his wife has heard one too many lame excuses (I had to shoot a night scene in Malibu/I had an important meeting in Malibu/Something happened in Malibu/I don't have to tell you everything). Also she doesn't much like being called a cunt. From his second wife, he will learn about cunnilingus, but he won't enjoy it, and they too will reproduce, a boy they name Seamus, and ten months later, a girl they name Erin (as in Go Bragh, which he thinks is hilarious one drunken night and briefly tries to convince his wife would make a great middle name, Right, she says, because I'm sure high school was a smashing success for Ima Hogg), but again, the drinking and cunt thing, so this marriage will also be short-lived. In 1972 he will land the role that will be the first line of his obituary, a wildly popular weepy drama (*Love Lives on Forever*) about a widower whose daughter dies of a rare disease but who finds love with her private nurse and learns to live again. For a while he pounds this costar as well, but she refuses his proposal. Mr. P, raised Catholic, has always believed in marriage, even though he doesn't know why and doesn't question why, even though the example set for him by his parents was not particularly inspiring (twin beds in his parents' bedroom, the door to which was almost always open/not much in the way of dinner conversation beyond Pass the green beans/not much in the way of motherly affection beyond a pat on the blanket after she'd tucked him in/Dad liked to drink and sleep with prostitutes). Still, he feels that there's something holy about it, marriage, or should be, at least; he believes this is the true and right thing for a man and a woman to do and is determined to find a wife he'll stick with one day.

After leaving the television producer, Mrs. P does a guest spot on an action series and quickly marries the star of the show, causing a sensation by hyphenating her last name. Her new husband doesn't much care for this, he's a bit of a traditionalist, but he's mad for her and takes it as part of the package. Frankly, he'd just as soon have her stay at home, which he lets her know on numerous occasions, to which she always says sweetly, some variation of, Oh . . . well . . . I don't think that's for me. In 1976 Mrs. P gets her big break on a new action series created with her in mind, this one featuring an all-female ensemble cast, for which her thick blond hair is cut to accentuate its natural wave, a hairstyle that will seemingly be copied by every woman in America for a time. It's around here that Mrs. P becomes acquainted with the tabloids, who declare that she is involved in everything from sex cults to sorcery. None of these things are ever true, and as much as she'd like her privacy back, a part of her wishes they'd go ahead and print the truth as she sees it, which is simply that she has the sex drive of an eighteen-year-old boy and likes to try new things (new things here including activity considered by some to be risky but which she sees as merely exciting and, perhaps most important, no one else's damn business). Because of the negative attention, Mrs. P cuts her hair into a pixie style (which looked good on Jean Seberg and, she realizes too late, only Jean Seberg, and which of course serves only to bring her more unwanted attention) and leaves the series that made her a star after just one season, and although her hair will be talked about for decades, she is not heard from again publicly until the '80s. Privately, between 1977 and 1983, several things happen, beginning with two miscarriages and three months in a private mental care facility—exhaustion is the reason made public, but in fact Mrs. P suffers a protracted and debilitating bout of depression brought on by the miscarriages, wonders if god thinks she'd be an unfit mother, wonders if she could love a child she didn't give birth to (she could, but will not find out), wonders if having a child would make her want to stay in one place (it won't), wonders if anything matters without children, which for a time leaves her profoundly hopeless about more or less everything else she'd previously cared about, even sex (What does it really mean, anyway, nothing). Intensive psychotherapy and brief affair with a yoga instructor help her to snap out of it, but all of it figures into, if not causes, the breakdown of her marriage.

Mrs. P's husband makes a serious miscalculation in introducing his wife to his best friend during this period, believing that his friend Mr. P will keep an eye on his unreliable wife while he's out of the country filming a made-for-TV movie about an

Australian bounty hunter. (I know she'll fuck somebody else if I leave her alone. Never met a woman or a man as horny as her in my life. And I've met a lot of women. And I'm horny.) What happens instead is that though Mr. P initially does remarkably well with this task, dissuading the future Mrs. P from a dalliance she's interested in having with a tile man doing work on her patio, Mr. P is thoroughly unable to resist her advances when they are made, and because they have begun to confide in each other during this time of their relationship troubles (He just doesn't get me/Women always leave me/Who would leave you, baby?/Ah I guess I can be a jerk sometimes), their bond is not merely sexual (especially given the initial absence of the cunnilingus Mrs. P is quite fond of), but as it turns out, a genuine connection that neither is prepared to give up. Mr. and Mrs. P talk about god and life (I just think, this can't be all of it, right? Like, stars? That can't just be explained by astroscience, right?/No, no way, baby/I know, right?) and even art (I'm completely taken with Matisse's colors/I can't say I know who that is/Here look at this book, baby, see, doesn't it just make you want to lay some paint down on the floor and roll around in it?/You are so fucking sexy, baby, I am over the moon for you), which is something Mrs. P has secretly been thinking about trying again someday, painting, and Mr. P says, If you were my wife, I'd build you a studio, and Mrs. P smiles and brushes it off as just a hobby, anyway, tells him he's sweet and changes the subject. Mr. and Mrs. P think these conversations are deep, even though they aren't, although who's to decide that, really, because they are with each other one hundred percent by now, and because they do really connect here, because they both feel something they haven't felt before, something they both believe no one has felt before, and maybe that's as deep as it ever needs to be. Mrs. P acquires a quickie divorce before her husband even returns to the country, and immediately moves in with Mr. P at his Beverly Hills mansion. Mrs. P's husband deals with this betrayal by waiting for a respectable ninety days before telling his side of the story to Barbara Walters.

Unsurprisingly, Mrs. P, in her soft-spoken way, her voice like a pot-smoking kitten, will inform Mr. P that he'll need to learn a few new tricks if he's interested in keeping her around. Mr. P makes a few initial stumbles but learns to please. In fact he learns a few extra tricks thanks to Mrs. P's interest in bondage and knife play. Some tricks he will flat-out refuse, like the time Mrs. P hears there's a new trend in Japan where people are utilizing electrically charged squid as one might use a dildo. (I'm not sure where the pleasure in that would be for me/It just goes where the dildo goes, honey/I don't think I want an electric sea creature shocking me up the ass/How will you know unless you try it?) He's about to say, I just do, but the look on Mrs. P's face is so inviting that she might be able to convince him that an atomic missile up his ass would be even better. For a time, this behavior will remain in the bedroom and will also involve weird third-person dialogue (Yeah, she loves his big dick in her mouth!/He's cumming! Mr. P is cumming! Here it comes!/Cum on her face!) and role-playing (teacher/underage student, pimp/drug-addicted whore, mommy/little boy, daddy/little boy [Mrs. P is always the daddy in this scenario; Mr. P is initially taken aback by this not because it's incestuous but because *it seems gay*, but it's another chance for Mrs. P to use a strap-on], priest/altar boy [a variation on the previous, with a few Biblical verses], brother/sister, farmhand/sheep).

For nearly a year, things are good, and outside of the bedroom they do a lot of the typical things couples do, travel, go to the movies, the beach, throw dinner parties (although admittedly, someone at their dinner parties always gets drunk enough to either break a large piece of furniture or punch someone). Once, on a leisurely hunt for beach glass, Mr. P gets down on one knee with the narrow end of a nicely sanded green beer bottle and places the glass ring on her finger, the look on his face as he proposes that of a puppy who just chewed up your grandmother's needlepoint pillow but still hopes to sleep in your bed. Mrs. P says, You're sweet, and resists the mysterious urge to pat him on the head, and tells him if she were to marry again, it would only be him, but he knows that tiny little *if* is the major problem with the entire sentence. Around this time, Mrs. P rescues a skinny calico kitten that shows up behind the air-conditioning unit, realizes, as she treats it for worms, lovingly salves its wounds, feeds it with a bottle, that her maternal instincts haven't abandoned her, perhaps even grew while she wasn't looking, and perceives an almost spiritual connection with the animal, would go so far as to say she feels not just appreciated but understood by the kitten, and is so moved by the experience that she begins donating large sums of money to animal-rescue groups. She has been asked to appear on behalf of various causes over the years, always declining but donating anonymously (Well, I just don't see why anyone needs to know, she'll say with a coy smile) and making no exception now. Mr. P, to date, has never gotten much more involved in anything terribly munificent outside of buying a few boxes of Thin Mints when the Girl Scouts come around, and has vocally disapproved of Mrs. P's inclinations in this area (You're going to go broke!/I have more than I need./You can't give to every pathetic person out there!/Yes, I can!), but has recently softened, partly in the hopes that it will make him seem more marriage-worthy (Will you marry me if I give a million dollars to sad dogs?/Maybe/Get me my checkbook).

With Mr. P's encouragement, Mrs. P will endeavor to get back in the acting game after a couple years absent, takes acting classes for the first time, finally auditioning for and landing a part in a feature as a woman whose child has been abducted. Around the time that Mrs. P's career begins to take off again, Mr. P's begins to take a nose dive, not crashing completely but forever remaining in middling comedies and the occasional cameo in a drama that shows the potential he had but never fully proved. It is during this period that Mr. and Mrs. P begin hurting each other. It could be argued that the origin of this behavior began with some of the sex play, but that remains uncertain. There is an incident when Mrs. P drips hot candle wax on Mr. P's testicles, which turns them both on for about a minute until Mrs. P accidentally drips a little too much and gives him a second-degree burn, which he believes she has done on purpose because she'd been angry with him about his unwillingness to try the squid. (Cunt! You know you meant to do that!/Why would I do that on purpose?/I don't know, maybe you see me as a father figure!/I don't need a father figure, my father's nice!/I bet he is, fatherfucker!/Maybe you were really fucking your father!/That doesn't even make any sense!/Don't you even say one more word about my daddy!/Fatherfucker!/ Well, maybe you were fucking your mother! Motherfucker!/ Bitch!/You're the little bitch!) This fight continues off and on for a good while, and will always be referred to in later fights. (You were supposed to pay the gardener/No you were supposed to pay the gardener/No my assistant was supposed to pay the gardener/Was the assistant supposed to read your fucking idiot mind?/Why are you so worried about the gardener anyway, do you want to fuck him?/Yeah, I'm a faggot now, I want to fuck the gardener/Hey, I don't know, maybe you do/Well maybe the gardener wouldn't burn me on the balls!/Let it fucking go, did you cum or not?) In any case, who throws the first punch is up for debate, but what is certain is that they're both throwing them. Mrs. P, being of a petite stature, does not inflict a lot of damage with her bare hands, but has great aim with pottery and is not afraid to throw it. After these incidents, there is always make-up fucking, and sometimes they're still bleeding, which makes them laugh. Sometimes they call each other Cunty and Motherfucker, affectionately. Several years later when Mrs. P leaves, it is not for this reason, but it may be the reason she comes back. In the summer of 1986 Mr. and Mrs. P conclude this period of their lives with the birth of their only child, Charlie, which as she'd long ago imagined, provides a meaning to her life that trumps everything else that matters to her, a meaning she tries unsuccessfully to explain to Mr. P, who feels something he doesn't care to call jealousy but looks a lot like it. (It's just . . . I feel . . . a knowing/A knowing./A knowing./ . . . /If you don't understand without me explaining, I don't think you're going to.) In spite of Mr. P's unknowing, the early years are magical, filled with trips to Disneyland and the redwoods and Maui, with playdates, Happy Meals, and bedtime stories. Mr. P sees Mrs. P bathing the infant boy in the kitchen sink, carefully soaping the baby's bald head, whisper-singing "Mockingbird," wrapping the baby in what looks to him like a velvet towel, and knows beyond doubt that he will never feel for another woman what he feels for this one. Mr. P, however, in spite of this example, will, on the occasion that he actually picks the baby up, continue to hold the boy as one might deliver the Thanksgiving turkey to the table, with about the same measure of pride, and as though the only purpose for lifting the boy is for the purpose of transporting him from one place to another. Mrs. P, the primary caregiver by a lot, will love the child as much as a child could be loved, but by the time he turns fourteen, he will have stolen and sold most of his mother's jewelry for drugs, wrecked a car he wasn't licensed to drive, and gone missing several times. An early excuse involving Malibu is not accepted, for obvious reasons. (I should have beat your ass with a yardstick like my father did/Yeah that worked out real good for you, Pops/ . . .)

Mr. P's relationships with his children have only rarely resembled anything falling on the positive side of the parenting scale. His relationship with his younger daughter, Erin, has never been good, considering that her mother moved her to the East Coast when she was six and he's visited her exactly four times in fifteen years, and has been strained even more ever since Erin decided that sex for any purpose other than procreation is a black sin and that her father will go to hell for it unless he accepts god, which Mr. P thinks is horseshit even though he considers himself to be a practicing Catholic, albeit one who sins and doesn't go to church. Mr. P tells his daughter that if he does go to hell, that'll be the least of the reasons. His son Seamus, now in his thirties, is a seventh-grade history teacher, the only P child to attend more than a semester at college, and who now has a family of his own, is by all accounts but his father's the well-adjusted one, perhaps due to the presence of a loving stepfather who entered his life early on, or perhaps just by luck of the draw, since this didn't seem to help his sister at all. No doubt Mr. P's hostility toward his son is exacerbated by Seamus's calm and easygoing demeanor. Seamus loves his father, but has learned from years of Al-Anon meetings to do so from a distance where there's no chance of being hit. Seamus sends his father and Mrs. P (whom all the P kids have always adored; You're too good for him/Why are you with him?/I love him/But why?/Why not?) birthday cards and holiday letters, calls a couple of times a month; Mr. P rarely offers any return communication, and rarely even returns Seamus's calls. When asked why by Mrs. P (or anyone for that matter), he says, I hate that guy, and that's all he ever says about it. Maggie, Mr. P's other neglected daughter, whose birthday he forgot every other year since she was five, endeavoring, unsuccessfully, to make up for it with cars and credit cards (She doesn't need a car, she's twelve/Well, did she like it?), is currently serving a three-year sentence at a women's prison for breaking and entering, a charge she pleaded no contest to on account of it being true; she had broken and entered her ex-husband's house and taken back her engagement ring, which she pawned for an ounce of black tar heroin. This causes Mr. P no small amount of anguish, which he deals with by smoking some black tar heroin. This, however, is not his drug of choice, so Mr. P adds to this some Percocet and Scotch, which leads to his third DUI arrest. Mr. P, who once had to pound milk shakes to keep his 150 pounds, still has his boyish looks, but has put on some weight and is puffy in the face from the drinking. He's thinking about an eye lift. Later he will get one, which will make his eyes look slightly inhuman, which he will attempt to remedy by adding eyeliner, which is one of those things some older men in Hollywood do that we shouldn't even try to understand. Mr. P is sentenced to ninety days of community service picking up trash on the 101 freeway, wearing dark sunglasses and the required pinny that in bold letters says LOS ANGELES DEPARTMENT OF CORRECTIONS, and during this time gives several autographs, which makes him happy and sad at the same time, which confuses him (as you might imagine, this inability to understand complexity of feeling has not aided him in his acting career either). Mrs. P leaves during this period, and even though there are plenty of obvious good reasons, it's not any of these. She just needs to go. She tries to explain this to Mr. P, that it's just a drive she has, that it doesn't have anything to do with him, and it doesn't, but he doesn't get it, and he's demolished, like when they fill up old buildings with dynamite and they're utterly flattened, like that, he tells her, flattened. He begs her not to leave, promises her anything she could possibly want, anything he could possibly do to make things work, couples therapy, liposuction, anything, but she just smiles, sadly, kisses his weird eyes and goes, takes troubled thirteen-year-old Charlie with her, and except for one horrendous incident with a prostitute, Mr. P will not get involved with anyone sexually or otherwise until they reunite. He will flirt a lot, in restaurants, in bars, in the grocery store, on the street, or his version of flirting (You ever see *Love Lives on Forever*? You want to?), mostly with women younger than his daughters, but none of this will result in sexual activity of any kind. Mr. P stalks Mrs. P a little bit periodically, moping in his car outside her house, showing up places he thinks she might be, leaving horrifically out-of-tune heartbreak songs on her answering machine (She's gone! Ain't no sunshine when she's gone! She's leaving! Leaving! On that midnight train to Georgia!) and sending sad, nonsensical letters (This period of my life, babe, is like smoke signals, and without you my mind goes to lunch), and she actually thinks it's kind of sweet, and she actually knows exactly what he means.

Mrs. P drops out of acting during this time, this time for good. She takes up painting and even though it's halfway decent, she doesn't get much in the way of critical acclaim, which she seems to understand (Yeah, it's a little they don't get it, a little "look at the girl with the hair having her fun"), but doesn't really care, because she sells a boatload of it. Also it fills her spirit, and in early 2002 she up and marries and quickly divorces a gallery owner. Needless to say, when Mr. P learns that she's married someone besides him, he calls her immediately and asks why she didn't just stab him in the stomach with a fire poker instead. Around here she watches a lot of *Oprah*, reads *The Road Less Traveled,* and starts listening to NPR, which she thinks is really interesting. She tells people, I just love learning, you know? even though she may not be fully comprehending the material being consumed. Often she learns things altogether wrong (Did you know that Kim Jong-il is responsible for the deaths of millions of babies in Taiwan?) or memorizes bits at the most basic level (The problems in our educational system can't be solved by throwing a bunch of money at it), nevertheless she's invigorated, and will tell anyone who will listen about the latest thing she learned.

In a blackout, Mr. P hears about the gallery guy on *Access Hollywood*, tracks him down, and kicks the shit out of him. Mr. P has never thought of his relationship with Mrs. P as abusive and neither has she. They always like to say *passionate* or *tumultuous*. They always like to say their love is one of a kind, even, or maybe especially, at times when they aren't technically together. We aren't really sure what to call it, *love* isn't the first word that comes to mind, but we haven't got another one. If you catch Mrs. P after she's heard this kind of scuttlebutt about her relationship, she'll say, Who are they to say what love is or isn't? You know what I think? I think love is easy. It doesn't mean you don't throw things at each other sometimes or take a few years off for yourself. Mrs. P gets word of what Mr. P's done (via the tabloids, which she of course doesn't read but is hard-pressed to overlook at the supermarket checkout) and dreamily tells her best friend how romantic she thinks this is. In truth, Mr. and Mrs. P have never really been out of touch since the split, Charlie being their excuse for multiple daily phone calls that go well beyond what time he should be picked up from his AA meeting, but there are things they don't discuss, or we should say she won't discuss, for obvious reasons. So but Mr. P gets word from her girlfriend that she was touched to hear he defended her honor so gallantly, and starts writing her love letters again, really sweet, if unsurprisingly odd and misspelled love letters (I love you like a bonfire loves a marshmallow), and Mrs. P finally answers him back and tells him that if he goes to rehab, she'll consider taking him back someday, even though rehab doesn't have much to do with it, she just wants a little more time. Mr. P goes to rehab, and it doesn't take the first time, or the second time, but it does take the third time, which coincides with him being around long enough to become ironically popular again, getting some interesting parts in independent films and finally a sitcom. Mr. P sends flowers and gifts to Mrs. P every week (picked out by her girlfriend because he's inclined to pick out antelope-sized arrangements and Elizabeth Taylor–type bling for her even though she prefers freesia and hardly wears jewelry at all), but it isn't until she hears from her friend that he has prostate cancer that she begins seeing him again. Mrs. P visits him every day in his room at Cedars-Sinai, even though they've been apart for some time. She won't have any of what the nursing staff is selling her in terms of visiting hours (but does so in her charming way—Oh, I'll be on my way in just a few, and then sleeps in his bed next to him for the length of his stay). Mrs. P also avails herself to Mr. P during his entire recovery, baking fresh berry scones every day, bringing flowers and reading *Anna Karenina* to him, mostly because Mrs. P has always loved the first line. (Usually, she just reads a page or two before he falls asleep.) Mr. P does everything he can to use his illness to get her to come back (I might croak tomorrow/Nice try, baby, the doctor says you're all clear/Ah, I don't know, I'm not feeling that great unless you're around/I'm always with you, baby, you should know that). Mr. P soon recovers and promises never to hurt Mrs. P again, and he doesn't.

Mr. and Mrs. P's son, Charlie, takes his turn in prison, also on drug-related charges. It's a terrible time for the Ps, much worse than the cancer, for Mrs. P the hands-down worst time in her life. Charlie doesn't blame her (prison dialogue, all family members present: Charlie, I should have done better by you, my sweet baby boy/Please don't blame yourself, Mom, I just got some shitty genes from Dad/So it's my fault/Yeah, well, you could have at least tried to make up the difference somehow/Did I not give you everything you needed? You live in our goddamn guest house with freaking maid service/Not now I don't/You're just an ungrateful little bitch/Stop it! Stop it right now!), but she can't help herself. At home, Mrs. P cries and cries, mostly alone in a secluded corner of her garden, until Mr. P finally pulls his head out of his ass and admits to her that he's fucked everything up with their kid, and that he wants to try to do right by her (Don't do it for me, baby, do it for him/I will, baby). Mr. P goes back to the prison without Mrs. P (for the first time) to see Charlie and weeping, confesses his sins.

(I've fucked all you kids up, I know it/Nah, Dad, the odds were against me in the womb/I still could have tried harder/You did the best you could, I know you got fucked the same way I did./I'm so, so sorry, Son/Hey, I thought love meant never having to say you're sorry/Yeah, that's a big load of horseshit/ (actual laughter here)/I want to do better now, if you'll let me try/Okay, Dad.) This particular *Okay, Dad* has any number of layers to it, including but not limited to total skepticism, lingering resentment he's too tired to express, and hope, a little tiny bit of hope that he might someday have a dad that acts like a dad, even now. Mrs. P, whose bright light is dimming just a bit now, leans on Mr. P, lets him stay over most nights now, and they no longer fight or throw anything, they make healthy dinners, watch movies, and have some sex that's a somewhat less energetic version of times past, but that has a tenderness that had never been there; Mr. P often lies quietly next to her after, while she falls asleep. He likes to say that he loves to watch her dreaming, he imagines, of kittens in palaces, dining on lobster rolls and ice cream sundaes, romping under rainbows and sleeping in canopy beds.

Mrs. P comes down with cancer herself, of the colon, unfortunately it is discovered rather late for anything but a miracle, which is what they both hope for, and now Mr. P tends to her. Mr. P shifts into a brand-new gear for this exercise, goes to great lengths to find a cure for his wife, learns to use the internet (for a while he hadn't even believed it existed; he would say, Who uses that really?, this around 2004), reads articles and calls around the world, everyone from doctors to shamans to the pope (the latter of whom is not easily reached for miracle-making, he discovers). He prepares most of her meals as smoothies because she can't tolerate solid foods and hardly has the energy to chew anyway. Mrs. P doesn't love all of these smoothies (I'm not crazy about the split pea, honey/Come on, it's just like soup, you love soup!/This is not like soup/Okay, sweetness, I'll fix you something different, what do you want, you name it/Chocolate banana/Okay baby, chocolate banana coming up/With whipped cream/You got it baby) but when he delivers them to her bed with a loopy straw and an edible violet blossom on top, she gives him a grateful, loving smile, albeit a cancer-stricken, half-lit version of her famous smile, a smile that makes him know his time on the planet hasn't been altogether useless. Mr. P gets down on his knees every morning and evening now, something he hasn't done since third grade, praying to god to cure Mrs. P, trying to make any deal he can think of, even some unsavory ones (Take me, take Seamus), weeping and even admitting some of his flaws (I know I'm a shitty father, I know I'm a dick in sixteen different ways, Mother Mary, but she's an angel, you probably already know that, and she doesn't deserve this, please don't take this out on her, she is good and kind and I don't think I can live without her). It is during this time that Mr. P makes the first of a number of marriage proposals that Mrs. P turns down. (Oh, silly, when are you going to stop asking me that?/When you say yes./I want to grow old with you./Sometimes I think people like me aren't supposed to grow old./What does that mean? What kind of people are you? Don't say that.) Mr. P thinks they're the same kind of people, the kind of people who like a good cheese and an old movie and who think too hard about the wrong things (which he thinks to say just in the moment, but which may be as insightful a thing that ever comes to him), who got lucky in the most important way when they found each other, the kind of people who are meant to grow old together, forever, until they're old and feeble and take an overdose of pills so they can die at the same time, in an embrace. This has been Mr. P's plan ever since he met Mrs. P. He knows there's not much time left but he still wants to be able to call her his wife, once and for all. (Please, baby, make me the happiest man in the world, we can do it however you like, a big church wedding, at the courthouse, I could rent a yacht, we can go to Vegas, whatever you desire/Oh I don't know.) But Mrs. P does know, she thinks maybe she's just meant to sparkle brilliantly for a short while and when the shine starts to dull, she'll just fizzle out quickly, like a bottle rocket.

Several days before her death, in a bit of a morphine haze but not at all unclear about her decision, Mr. and Mrs. P are married. She has mere days left, so it's hardly as he always imagined, an all-white barefoot ceremony on the beach, close friends (and even some family), vows they wrote themselves, Mrs. P with a single gardenia behind her ear. The only thing that's white in reality is the harsh fluorescent lights above them, and the only people present besides them are the hospital chaplain, an uninvited nurse who randomly walks in with a handyman, insisting that one of the monitors needs to be checked at this exact moment, and Mrs. P's best girlfriend as a witness. Mrs. P has, with the doctor's permission, cut her morning dose of morphine in half, but is still drowsy and in pain and distracted by a fly buzzing around her head. At Mrs. P's request her friend has dabbed a tiny bit of rose lipstick on her lips and cheeks, and Mr. P has brought a gardenia for her hair, which she uses for a bouquet instead, because she loves the fragrance, says the fragrance is so heavenly that when she closes her eyes for a second it positively takes her away. The chaplain weds them with the traditional vows, although Mrs. P's not listening at the moment, Mr. P smiles and snuffs and makes a slashing motion across his neck when the chaplain says "obey," her friend gives a small inaudible chuckle, and although Mrs. P has been unable to prepare anything, Mr. P has with him the dog-eared, folded-up vow he's been hanging on to since he wrote it thirty years ago. Tears run down his puffy face as he reads it, the others in the room are welling up too, all but Mrs. P who's in and out, and returns only long enough to see Mr. P wiping away tears and telling her that he knows he's still not a very good man, but she's made him a better one, and that fourteen lifetimes from now when he's an armadillo and she's a gazelle, he will still love her as much as he does this day, as much as always.

At the funeral, Mrs. P's bereaved, ninety-two-year-old father is led down the aisle, held tightly by Mr. P on one side and Charlie on the other, because he can barely stand from the grief. He asks Mr. P, weeping, not expecting an answer, Why her, I'm an old man, why not me? Why my sweet angel girl? Mr. P says he's not sure his wife was really made for this world. Mr. P's father considers this for a moment before he speaks. What world do you suppose she was made for, then? I don't know, Mr. P says. A better one.

Best Friends Seriously Forever

Somewhere in Louisiana there are two fourteen-year-old best friends who like to go swimming in a river near where they live where there used to be no alligators but then there were. Mandy and Terri are swimming in the river as usual in their new bikinis from Target, splashing and talking about the two cute brothers who just moved down the street who are splashing and horsing around about ten yards away from them and who are for sure coming to the Taco Bell tonight (another place where they like to go) because they look so foxy in their new bikinis from Target. Mandy and Terri are about to go dry off with their Hello Kitty and 'N Sync beach towels, respectively, when Mandy slips on the muddy bank and screams that she's stuck in something, thinks maybe it's a sharp tangle of roots not yet knowing that what she's stuck in is an alligator until she sees its eyes and head emerge from the muck with her thigh fully clamped in its jaw. Mandy screams, It's an alligator! Terri pulls at Mandy and at the same time yells, Alligator! Alligator! Mandy's stuck in an alligator! over to the two cute brothers who run out of the water and don't put on their flip-flops even and who for a second look like they're running over to save Mandy from the alligator but then they keep running and it becomes clear that they are running home and away from alligators altogether. Terri has to take drastic measures now and almost as though she has superhuman powers, pounds the alligator on the head, startling it enough for her to pry open its mouth, and screams at Mandy, Get out, Mandy, now! Mandy, go, Mandy, get out, get out! so that Mandy can get out and Mandy gets out and runs out of the river and so does Terri. Mandy is hurt pretty bad, Terri doesn't want to even tell her how bad her chomped leg looks, or what those giant teeth looked like, like there were a thousand of them all dripping with mud and her best friend's blood. In a minute they'll go to the hospital but right this minute Mandy and Terri have collapsed into a fit of giggles about overcoming the alligator. At the hospital Mandy and Terri are interviewed for the local news and Mandy says, Terri is my best friend? And always was my best friend? But now is seriously my best friend? And will be my best friend seriously forever? and when they ask if she was scared Terri says, I didn't even think about it really, I was just trying to get Mandy out. Mandy and Terri grow up and don't stay best friends seriously forever but not because they forget. They don't forget so much as move away and lose touch the way people do. They just get married and move away and have babies and sort of forget, but not totally. When their kids are old enough to go swimming they swim only in pools and Mandy and Terri think of each other at these times and tell their husbands that they once escaped an alligator and the husbands only believe them when they show them the yellow newspapers and when Mandy and Terri look at the yellow newspapers is when they remember.

Old Friends

Back in New York at her house, we slept a little late. We showed each other all our new clothes and we remarked on how stylish and how evolved we were, emotionally. We took our time going out; there was nothing new I needed to see. We went to lunch at Alice's Tea Cup where we had tea sandwiches. Mine were cucumber and watercress. Then we went shopping and got lingerie for a good price. In our haste, some of it was knocked off the displays; giggling occurred. Then we came home and sat around and ate black and white cookies and played with the cat. Then we Google-imaged all the ex-boyfriends we could think of. We couldn't think of all of them because sometimes we could only remember their nicknames, like Pink Man, On My Nerves, and The Village Idiot. Most of them had become old, except for the one I hate the most, who still had all his hair.

Justin Bieber's Hair in a Box

Justin Bieber's hair is in a box on your dresser, a gift for your niece: Justin Bieber's hair, in a small clear box, on your dresser, next to your necklaces and your spare change and your hairbrush. Justin Bieber's hair is glad to be here. Justin Bieber's hair wants you to open the box and let it out, wants to spend your spare change on gum and candy, wants to try on your necklaces and brush itself. Justin Bieber's hair can see what you see out your window, sees your vision of the world and likes it. Justin Bieber's hair sees you there and likes what it sees. Justin Bieber's hair has a great personality, you would know this if you let it out of the box. Justin Bieber's hair would do your dishes for you, wouldn't you like that? Justin Bieber's hair believes that age is just a number, just like you're always saying! Justin Bieber's hair has no stance on abortion. Justin Bieber's hair is so soft and smells so good, you should really let it out of the box. Justin Bieber's hair thinks you look so pretty today. Justin Bieber's hair knows what you want. Justin Bieber's hair wants to touch you. Justin Bieber's hair will hold you afterward. Justin Bieber's hair wants to be whatever you want it to be, if you'd just give it the chance. Justin Bieber's hair wants nothing more than to love you.

Stella's Thing

1. Stella had two tattoos: a bee on each clavicle, bee-sized. It hurt when she got them. Her boyfriend at the time kept bees on the roof of his building in Queens.

2. At the time.

3. The bee tattoos kind of always hurt, a little bit. It's totally fair to say they stung. We're not trying to be funny about it.

4. Then her boyfriend wasn't her boyfriend but she still had two bee tattoos. That's how tattoos work. *What do I do about these bees*, she said to her friend Zae. *Cover them up!* Zae said. Zae had a lot of tattoos. *Do you know how many ex-lovers are under here*? Stella said no. *A shit ton, man. A shit ton*. Her friend laughed. *But they hurt so much in the first place*, Stella said. *Yeah, man*, Zae said. *That's what tattoos* are, she said, smiling.

5. Tank top season was coming and the bees were still stinging but Stella didn't want to have to look in the mirror and think of her ex-boyfriend every day, so she walked to the closest tattoo parlor and picked out a couple of butterflies. She

knew it was a little bit of a cliché, didn't think she really needed transforming, but the butterflies were pretty, and blue, and just big enough, and fuck that guy and his bees.

6. Weirdly, the tattoos stopped stinging after that.

7. Moths, Zae said. *Interesting choice. What?* Stella said. *They're butterfries. Butterflies.* Stella was a little bit stoned. *No, those are moths. Huh,* she said, looking down at them. *Well, I still like them.*

8. Stella got a lot of compliments on her new tats that summer. She felt sexy and free of the bee man.

9. Then it was fall. Cardigan season. Stella had been collecting vintage cardigans since she was in high school. So almost six years. But she knew how to find really good ones for cheap. And no, she won't tell you where. Well, she might. But probably not.

10. Mostly she was into men's cardigans from the '50s and '60s, women's if she was feeling a certain way. But mostly men's.

11. The smaller ones were hard to find. Plus Stella was pretty small herself. Even the small ones were oversized. But there's oversized and then there's oversized.

12. Occasionally, Stella would take a chance on putting one through the wash to shrink it up, but only if it was over-over-sized. The first time this worked out perf. After, mixed results. *Why do you keep doing that when you know it always comes out like a sweater for a misshapen baby,* Zae said. Stella said *Because of the purple one.* Zae said *Oh yeah. That one is super good.*

13. The cardigans were known to be Stella's thing.

14. She was actually thinking of opening a shop.

15. *Do you think anyone would come to a shop that just sold one thing, though?* she asked her friend. *There's a shop in Paris that only sells umbrellas*, Zae said. Stella imagined this in her head, pictured Paris with nothing but shops that sold one thing. *We should move to Paris*, she said. *We can't afford Paris*, Zae said. *We can barely afford it here.*

16. Stella and Zae worked together at Buffalo Exchange.

17. *What are we even doing with our lives?* Stella asked.

18. *I dunno, man,* Zae said. *I can't think about that right now.*

19. Stella was thinking about it a little right then. She was twenty-four. Meaning: nearly thirty.

20. Stella was hanging some clothes in a dressing room for a customer when she caught sight of the holes in her sweater, one of her favorites, with blue and yellow stripes. It was the perfect length. *Aw, man,* she said. They were kind of big, as holes go. She took it off and tossed it in the back room, borrowed another one off the rack. She wasn't stoked about it. Stella looked at every last cardigan that came into that store before they went onto the rack. It was rare that she put one on the rack that she had wanted to buy for herself.

21. This was maybe part of why she could barely afford it here.

22. By the end of the workday, there were holes in her borrowed sweater. *You're going to have to pay for that*, the manager

said. Stella put her old sweater back on before they left. *Whoa,* Zae said. *They're like, right over your ink. The holes.*

23. It was about a half dozen sweaters in before Stella added it up. A person doesn't go right to moth-tattoo-is-eating-holes-in-my-sweaters.

24. By this time, though, Stella had begun wearing only her polyester sweaters, which were fewer in number by far. They were cute, but they were clammy. Nobody likes a clammy sweater.

25. *What the hell should I do?* Stella asked her friend. *You could get them covered up,* Zae said.

26. Stella thought it through and pictured the old lady who swallowed a fly, ending with giant horse tattoos across her entire chest.

27. In a darker mood, Stella considered other options. *Cotton? Just shirts? I get cold so easily. Nah, man,* Zae said. *You should just make it your thing. Sweaters with holes?* Stella asked. *Why not?* Zae said. *It's nobody else's thing.*

28. Stella spent some time after this thinking about what her thing really even was, whether she ever had a thing that was really hers. Other people wore cardigans. Were cardigans with holes enough of a thing to be her real thing? Her forever thing?

29. Not so much. Forever itself was the opposite of her thing.

30. Stella typed *sweaters with holes* into Google image search. She wasn't sure what she was looking for. She saw, of course, images of sweaters with holes, but she also saw some

other images. That's what Google is. She didn't have to scroll down far to learn about darning.

31. Darning was definitely a thing.

32. Maybe one of the most beautiful things Stella had ever seen.

33. Stella watched some tutorials on YouTube and taught herself to darn.

34. *You should maybe use polyester yarn, just sayin',* Zae told her. *Genius, Stella said.*

35. Zae ordered Stella a vintage darning egg from etsy. It had layers of paint partly worn off it from use. Stella cried. *It's so smooth*, she said.

36. *I really do want to open a shop,* Stella said. *You should,* Zae said. *How do you open a shop?* Stella asked. *Beats the hell out of me,* Zae said. *Maybe ask somebody who has a shop.*

37. Stella walked into a shop that sent her to another shop that sent her to another shop that sent her to a gallery in Rockaway Park.

38. It took a long time to get there from where she lived.

39. The gallery in Rockaway Park was kind of just a street-level apartment. The lady there told her she could use one room for 450 bucks a month, month-to-month, one month security. But the room faced the sidewalk and it had a window and she could see one of her sweaters hanging there, in her mind.

40. Stella so didn't have nine hundred dollars.

41. Zae said, *I'll give you what I have*. She pulled her wallet

out of her back pocket. It had a picture of a dog sniffing another dog's butt on it and seventeen dollars inside.

42. Stella cried again. *You're such a good friend.*

43. *Stop crying*, Zae said.

44. Stella bought some yarn with some of the money and smushed the rest into a vintage medicine bottle she kept on her dresser. There was maybe another seventeen dollars in there. Stella didn't believe in banks. She knew she wasn't going to collect the rest of the nine hundred dollars anytime soon, but at least she couldn't get it out without breaking the bottle.

45. Stella really didn't want to break the bottle.

46. Stella darned the holes in her sweaters. She chose colors that one might say didn't go with the colors of the sweaters.

47. Things that went with other things were not Stella's thing.

48. Stella had always known what wasn't her thing much more than what was. This seemed like maybe it was the most her thing so far.

49. Zae came over to Stella's after work to look at her inventory. It was impressive. *This is like, so much more than a thing. This is like, a brand*, Zae said. *I don't think I'm ready for a brand*, Stella said. Zae shoved a five-dollar bill into Stella's bottle. *I think you're my thing*, Stella said. *Do not cry*, Zae said. *Jesus. Hey, no offense, Stell, but this place is a dump.*

50. Stella didn't take it personally. It was a two-bedroom and she had four roommates and one of them had loud sex and

two of them had cats but no one had a vacuum cleaner or even replaced the can of Febreze Stella had bought after it ran out. That was four whole bucks.

51. *Where am I gonna go, though?* Stella made nine dollars and seventy cents an hour. *Maybe you could live in that room in Rockaway. That is the most genius thing ever*, Stella said. Stella called that lady back right away.

52. Stella moved to Rockaway. She hung her best sweater in the window. No one came in for a while. There wasn't a ton of foot traffic. She sold one to a rando off the street for a hundred bucks once and he let her Instagram it. She hashtagged that right up, and got 146 hearts. That was exciting. Then it was quiet again for a while.

53. Zae came to visit and bought one of Stella's sweaters and they walked on the beach.

54. *Let me tell you what,* Stella said to Zae. *The beach? Is for sure my thing. Right on,* Zae said.

55. Anyway, this wasn't that long ago. So we don't really know how it's going to turn out. Probably, this won't be the rest of her life. Does it have to be?

Notes for an Important American Story

This is a story about a man whose heart is large but full of rage. Or just angst. Or just malaise. Something like that. It is set on a sweeping piece of land in West Virginia or New Mexico, or at a small Midwestern university with financial problems, or during the apocalypse, or post the apocalypse, or maybe Brooklyn. The state of the world has rendered him powerless and apathetic. Maybe he has everything he thought he wanted but feels nothing. That could be good. Something to do with his father. Or his mother. Or both. Often he drinks too much. Often his angst presents as compulsive, near-violent masturbation. Someone may have committed suicide, probably his mother. This man might ride horses or he might be a washed-up academic. He might have an alienated teenage son, or an alienated adult son whose life he has ruined. Possibly the son comes back to town seeking reconciliation but instead they have a fistfight. The scope of the man's ability to ruin lives is wide, and he can do it with a fist or with a casual remark. This man hates himself, but has a cunning knack for directing his self-hate toward those around him in just such a way that it takes them a while to realize it.

He will need to have at least one brother. This is not a man with sisters. The man and his brother(s) will need to compete. It may be about a woman or about how one is favored or adopted or they may not even know what about. Any brother should be damaged in some way.

He might have a secret, but not necessarily. He could wear everything on his sleeve.

He does not have a feminine side. Or he totally does and this is his problem. He's failed his father in this way. By not going into the military. Or the family business.

He smokes, and has no interest in quitting, or tries repeatedly and always fails.

Perhaps he makes subtly racist or sexist or homophobic remarks on occasion, but sees himself otherwise, mostly on account of having fucked that Asian gal or that one guy that one time. Somehow this all relates to politics. Or war. Terrible things he's seen or done. Or philosophy. Terrible things he's thought about.

He is handsome, maybe in a rugged way, maybe in a soft way. If he's handsome in a soft way, wide eyes and a sort of cheeky thing, he will spend no small amount of time obsessing about this failure of birth, and attempts to compensate in a variety of ways, sexually, academically, etc. It's possible that his entire persona is a result of this compensation. Above all he has charm. Killer charm. In the big-budget-film version of his story (from which he will publicly distance himself), he'd be played by George Clooney.

There's a beautiful woman in his life; she exists only on a marble pedestal he has constructed for her with the express purpose of knocking her off it. This is a woman whose beauty defies the very meaning of beauty. Her beauty is heretofore unseen, as if beauty didn't really even exist before. It's a beauty that transcends description, but if he were to try, she would for sure have hair the color of a newborn colt shining under the light of a thousand suns, she would have skin like alabaster silk, lips the color of spilled blood. She would have eyes a brand-new color, like kaleidoscopes, where if you looked into them, you would see a perfect world.

Theoretically, she is there to reflect him back to himself for some learning. But not too much. Maybe just enough so that he understands something about himself on an even deeper level, but not so much to change his ways. His ways should remain unchanged. Maybe he's more of a metaphor than a man, whatever that means.

Truthfully, the woman is pretty, but not that pretty. Who is? She's pretty enough to have modeled in one JCPenney ad when she was nine, smart enough at nine to have immediately rejected a career based on image. Her greatest asset is her brain, but he'll never truly know this. He thinks he will, but for him it's still 99.9 percent biology, which is also the source of some angst, because he's smart enough to feel he should be able to overcome that, but also aware that he's not willing to really try, and also aware that he sort of doesn't have to try, because he's attractive and successful enough to where his brains and charm push him over into "extremely attractive to a lot of women." Anyway, whatever it is that she's got, he wants. They meet at a saloon where she tends bar, or in a classroom (she is his student; she is always his student) or on the set of a movie, one that isn't very good; he may have been nominated for an Oscar as a young man in the '70s, now he's playing the family patriarch. She's working craft services while finishing her undergrad at Columbia (she dropped out in the '90s). He notices she's reading a book of poetry, one he's read before; they talk. He's actually married, though they've been living apart for some time, and she knows he's married, and this is so not her thing, married men (famous married men!), whether or not they're apart, though cheating is sometimes his thing, and he will continue to feel her out. Part of the thing is he's not really picking up on what she's putting out, which is, initially, basically nothing. She's friendly to everyone, and maybe even more friendly to someone who chats her up about poetry. But that's it. Would she be attracted to him if he weren't married? Maybe? Sure? Yes, but believes she can shut that down when someone's married? But actually who is she kidding? So maybe there's a tiny vibe of that that he could be picking up, or thinks he's picking up, but really isn't enough to hang anything much on, even though that's exactly what he'll do.

This is when the wooing begins, small at first, he has calculated that she is ordinarily not one to date a married man, so maybe he'll bring a used book he thinks she might like, "just a loaner," something that wouldn't have to be construed as wooing, a text message, not even flirty, doesn't matter, he knows what he's doing, slowly building up to grander gestures, throwing a brand-new carton of cigarettes out the window because she mentions she hates it, maybe her mother died of lung cancer, maybe he steals her away to Battery Park to look at the sunset even though he's supposed to be on set and holds up the production for an hour, until finally he wears her down, just a tiny bit, whispers compliments in her ear about how her mind drives him crazy, how there's a *potent* connection between them, and how can she just ignore that, and so in spite of her better judgment, she lets him take her away for a weekend at his house in Bucks County and that's it. He's a movie star and he's sexy as hell and he reads poetry and she has come to believe that he sees something in her that maybe she hasn't seen in herself, which may or may not be true, because one of his skills is making you think things he wants you to think. *You* here being "women he's interested in."

So she goes, and they spend most of the weekend in bed, and the sex will either be on the rough side or on the tender side, or maybe even on the underwhelming side, it almost doesn't matter, because she allows herself to like him for a minute, and this minute, of course, is an important minute, a minute in which something is lost, something here being his interest. They return from their weekend in Bucks County, he kisses her good-bye like, That was amazing, looks into her eyes like, I am going to come to your place tonight or maybe you could even stop by my trailer so I can fuck you again good, but that's it, the last look like that, and don't forget he's an actor, he can toss a look like that in his sleep, but about a hot minute after this look happens, he's not hanging around the craft table anymore, if he bothers returning her texts they're short and usually irrelevant to her text; Coffee later? will be answered with a series of punctuation marks, something like an emoticon she's never seen before. She recognizes what's happening immediately, of course, because she's a bright gal, and quickly regains her better judgment, and backs off, tells him, *Okay, that was fun, let's call it a day.* Before she gets in too deep. This will of course respark his interest a bit, and he will endeavor to keep her just interested enough for a while, and will put in the most marginal effort, bringing flowers from the Korean market, talking just a little bit about the future, not a fully committed future where they own a house together but maybe a future vacation, a play he thinks she should see, or he'll say, *My mom would really like you, you should meet her,* something just enough to plant a seed, good enough for a brief delay, and he'll of course sleep with her a few more times, until she endeavors to bring up a conversation about how this doesn't really work for her, and he tells her that he let her know from the beginning that he was never really available, and she tells him that in fact that was not at all what happened, that he pursued her as though he was totally available, and then he has to resist the urge to point out that everyone knows he's married, because he knows he'll look like a dick if he assumes that everyone knows about his personal life because he's famous, even if it's true, but still he convinces her to go for a drive in the country, talk things through, she's pretty weary by now but agrees to go, and they stop and fuck at the first motel they pass, and the car ride back is rather silent, because she's done. This will set off a period in which the movie star more or less stalks her, which seems kind of crazy, right, last week he was finished with her, plus he's a movie star and could have anyone he wants, seemingly, but of course it's not very often that someone seems not to want him, and after the movie ends he will start writing her long, often incoherent letters, probably written drunk, and he will leave so many messages, alternating between desperate, a little bit sweet, and verbally abusive, to where she will change her phone number. He will never divorce or get back together with his estranged wife, but at her funeral, he will again wonder if they should have tried to work it out.

The beautiful woman will repeat this process with another man, another man not at all unlike our hero the movie star, this time a brilliant professor (hers, as noted) who is technically available in that he isn't married, but one who's never quite recovered from a sex scandal that in fact hadn't happened, or hadn't happened the way it was portrayed and/or gossiped about, or in his mind wasn't any kind of a scandal, it was a private affair between two consenting adults, never mind that one of them had only just voted for the first time and the other had just turned forty. Though he was cleared of all charges of sex with a minor, the damage to his reputation was done. None of this comes to her attention, she sees only that he smokes an awful lot of pot and is perhaps overly interested in talking about pot, is extremely knowledgeable about pot, and different kinds of pot, and is thinking about getting involved in the legalization of pot, except for he's usually too busy smoking it kind of all day, seems kind of depressed and doesn't want to socialize much, but still they have long conversations on his porch or her front stoop into the night, and he too has this thing where he knows how to perfectly balance his profusely expressed awe of her with enough subtle but diminishing comments whereby she might as well literally be performing a gymnastic act of walking this balance for the duration. He'll tell her that her particular type of beauty is underappreciated, but that he's the man for the job.

But then later there's a guy who appears to be totally different. So different that at first she's not interested. Maybe she's not really attracted to him, maybe he's in advertising but not in creative, in like accounts payable or something. Maybe the fact that she's not really attracted to him is part of the reason she gives him a chance, maybe she's just trying to be open. Maybe she thinks a less attractive, ordinary-seeming guy with an ordinary job will have ordinary issues, or maybe no issues, and she could grow to love him. And but what she doesn't bank on is that she will grow to love him (*love* here being, well, maybe not the perfect word, *desire* could be more appropriate, it's hard to say whether love is just this pure thing that isn't ever complicated, or is definable more than one way, or definable by each individual or each couple, sometimes you think you know what it is by what it isn't, or what it shouldn't be, like any of the scenarios depicted here in these notes so far may not seem like love to you, but who's to say if it works for you, what it is, really? If you fight and fight and fight and you fuck and fuck and fuck and laugh and laugh and laugh and you stay together forever, is it love? Or what if you just do all that for a period of years and then it's over? Was it not love because it ended? Does anybody know?). So anyway, they spend time together and it turns out he's kind of an interesting thinker, he'd taken some philosophy classes in college, and they have long conversations over many bottles of wine that make her reconsider a lot of ideas she had about the world that were sort of fixed, but then at some point the overall vibe of these conversations seems to take a turn into the-world-is-a-terrible-place kind of thing, which ties back into why he's really at this job, because he's just passing time until he dies, because there's not much point to anything, and it doesn't really matter what anyone does because the world is self-destructing. She asks—facetiously—why he doesn't just kill himself, and he says because he's a coward, and she spends some time trying to pep-talk him (resisting her urge to explain just now that suicide isn't generally thought of as an act of bravery), spends a lot of time trying to convince him of the world's good, gives him a ton of examples of the small beauties and goodnesses in the world, like his eight-year-old niece who excitedly collects pennies for UNICEF (*A pointless exercise*, he says), or the barista who always smiles and lets the line back up every day to make him his latte exactly how he likes it (*She just wants a tip*), or how much his dog lives for his existence (*Well, sure, I feed him*), tells him that he can contribute, make it better, but this is futile, and eventually they break up too. As with the academic, and the movie star, this goes back and forth for just a little while until he is sure he can be the one to break it off last. The last time he won her back involved actual threats of suicide, which was a pretty brilliant (if profoundly fucked-up) plan on his part, especially because she'd actually mentioned it, because it played into her hidden desire for this kind of power, that her love was so powerful that she could actually save the life of a man, in spite of a sort of logical voice in the back of her head that told her (a) how totally fucked that was and (b) that he was, as he'd said, never really suicidal at all.

After several go-arounds, the beautiful woman decides it's easier to let him be the one to break it off than to put the effort in. Also there's a whole thing about being the break-upper or the break-uppee, and how a person is one or the other, and she has accepted herself as the break-uppee partly because it's easier to think of yourself as not the bad guy this way, although then you admittedly sometimes end up thinking of yourself as the victim, which is really not any much better. It may even be worse.

Finally the beautiful woman meets a guy who seems to be everything she's looking for. He's an artist, he's engaged with the world, he's not depressed, and he's madly in love with her. There's no conflict above and beyond whatever any good couple might have whereby no two people live their lives exactly the same way and so you just sort of pick your battles kind of thing, and let stuff like socks on the floor go, where with someone else who makes you want to pull your hair out, socks on the floor might be a deal breaker. Everything is amazing for a while until he's offered a full-time job in Marfa that comes with a 12,000 SF studio. This guy is so great that he genuinely puts this forward as a discussion, that if living in Marfa is something she thinks she just can't do, he'll let the opportunity go. They even go to Marfa and look at houses, it's actually quite charming, there's much to like and they could live extremely well there, though it's more than a bit isolated. But she can't do it. She feels awful about it but she just feels like, love of her life or not, she can't see herself living in Texas, even in an arty town, for the rest of her life. She had lived in Texas for two miserable years in high school when her parents were separated, couldn't reconcile the absence of real seasons, couldn't get comfortable with the sounds of nature year-round, like she liked nature fine, at designated times, like in the summer, or at her grandparents' house where the sound of mourning doves or cicadas seem to fit, but year-round the sound of mourning doves is disconcerting, and in the city she might complain about the sounds of traffic or the sounds from the sports bar next door or a jackhammer or a fight on the street too, but at least those sounds make sense to her. She's a New York City girl, a freelancer, and except for those two years in Texas she never lived anywhere else. She could work anywhere really, and his job will more than cover their living expenses, and in Marfa, with no obligations, she could even work on that book she's been wanting to start. But she tells him she doesn't think she can do it, and he says, *Okay, then, we'll stay.* Which is when she tells him to go without her. Which is when she realizes how much worse it really is to be the bad guy. Which is when she realizes she's got as many problems as all the guys she's dated prior to this nice guy and she finally goes off and gets some therapy because enough of this shit already. It takes a few years but she gets her shit together, goes to graduate school, gets a teaching job herself, and that's it. Maybe does or maybe doesn't meet another genuinely stable nice guy. Either way, not very interesting, this ending. Better you should go watch *An Unmarried Woman* at this point.

There might be some redemption in the end. Perhaps religion has been the origin of our movie star's ruin, but may also provide his salvation. Salvation could even have come via his good woman if he'd given her a chance, not by most-likely-fake suicide prevention but just in that way that a really good relationship brings out the best in you without seeming to even be an effort on anyone's part but just because you're right for each other. That's not this story. They weren't right for each other and there probably isn't any right person for him, or there is, or there's more than one but he's just not willing to let it happen, and so he will keep looking but he will think about the beautiful woman long after she has found a right person. He might even convince himself she was the right person, the only right person, and that he blew it big time when he let her go, because that would be a good reason not to ever commit to an actual right person. Later he develops some health problems, his heart most likely, will end up in a nursing home with a bunch of old people, still miserable though there is a cute night nurse he flirts with when he can't sleep, which is most of the time. She's about thirty years younger than him, happily married, had no idea he was a famous movie star/academic/whatever until he told her, still doesn't know who he is, just wants to make his end a little more pleasant, maybe even succeeds. Maybe she's the last person to squeeze his hand and when he goes, he takes that hand squeeze with him to heaven or hell or wherever he's going, and that hand squeeze is now the only thing that's ever really mattered, or it's all the things that ever mattered, to him or to anyone. To everyone.

Maybe this story isn't American enough. Or maybe it's already been told. Or maybe it's a novel.

If it is, it has an amazing last line.

Heroes

Ask Nate Pinckney-Alderson, age six, what he wants to be when he grows up, and he will say, *I want to be a superhero.* Ask him which one, like his parents did, *Batman, Spider-Man, Wolverine, Cyclops?* and Nate Pinckney-Alderson will say, *Bob Brown*, and if you look at him like, Bob who? Nate will say again, *Bob Brown*, with yet another dramatic and exasperated sigh, *The superhero who saved the kid from the bus*. Nate's parents, remembering the man from a recent local news story, consider explaining the difference between a hero and a superhero, but quickly realize that it's a pretty good kid who wants to model himself after a real person he admires.

In fact, Nate has, since birth, had the ability to dream of actual crimes before they happen, but since there's no way for him to know this right now (he knows only that he wakes up screaming on an almost-nightly basis), there's also no way for him to put this superpower to good use.

Turning now to this Bob Brown, to say that he is an average guy is to flatter him. It's true, you'd be unlikely to notice him on the street—Bob Brown has a wardrobe of polo shirts primarily in unnatural-seeming shades of blue, and rotates a couple pairs of polyblend chinos; he's also been wearing the same style of Rockports since 1989 that he special-orders from an outlet store, and although he has the good sense not to style his thinning hair into a comb-over, he's got a lone, slight, unfortunate puff of it in the center of his forehead that there's really no good solution for.

The thing about Bob Brown and why he's not average is because he's not really very nice. He's not the kind of guy who turns into a murderer and then when they interview the neighbors they're all, *Oh, I'm so shocked, I never would have guessed!* He's the kind of guy, who, should he turn into a murderer and they interview his neighbors, they all have stories about how he always puts his trash bins in front of their garage door (and then defends his actions by shrugging and saying *Sorry* in such a way that it is very clear that he is the opposite of sorry) or always plays loud world music (and then defends his actions by saying he's *bringing culture to the neighborhood*) or always letting his lawn grow in, to the point where it would more appropriately be referred to as a field except for the fact that it's lawn-sized (and then defends his actions however he pleases in the moment—*It's fuel-efficient, it's natural, this is my aesthetic*). Mr. Brown's not-niceness comes in a lot of *always*. Even his friends have *always*es, and also some *never*s (always sends sarcastic text messages, never returns calls), and some *always/never* combos (always says he'll come to your party/help you move/give you a ride, but then never shows up), to the point where it's hard to believe he has any friends at all (he has one from grade school, one from high school, and one from work, and none of them are very nice either—they bond a lot over shared grievances relating to what's wrong with everyone besides them), or a wife, who has her complaints as well (he always uses the word *stupid* to describe her actions, never tries very hard to please her sexually once he's been pleased himself).

So when Bob Brown one day is waiting at the stop at Western and Belmont for his bus home from work (Bob teaches physics at Lane Tech—he's not a bad teacher at all, but he's perpetually cranky, and is frequently ridiculed behind his back or in illustrated notes passed in class), and a kid wearing his pants down around his butt to where he has to hold on to them while he's running or even just walking (Bob is not a fan), except this time he is running, and bumps hard into this other kid, a much littler kid, sending him into the street in front of the oncoming bus, Bob does what you assume most people would do (or maybe not, since no one else does right then), which is to run out after the boy and push him out of the way. Via the grateful parents of the little kid and the amazed onlookers, the media quickly latches on to this story as the uplifting one they use at the end of the broadcast to try to make everyone forget the rest of the show, and for a brief time Bob Brown is celebrated as a hero.

Nate, as of late, has been endeavoring to save lives to the best of his ability. Unfortunately, still completely unaware of his superpower, Nate has begun to assemble outfits that fall less than authentically into the style of Bob Brown, insofar as the hues of blue are more muted, his chinos are 100 percent cotton, and also he has taken the liberty of adding a cape that his mother fashioned for him from a remnant of blue velvet and some gold fringe trim patched onto the back to read BB. Regardless of the authenticity of the overall look and the fact that he is endlessly teased on the playground, Nate feels empowered by this garb and has been keeping his eyes open lately for crimes in progress or babies in jeopardy, but the reality of his life in first grade is such that it just doesn't come up that much. Hypervigilant now, though, Nate begins pushing kids away from anything he remotely perceives as harm—a lowering teeter-totter, a pair of snow boots propelled by a fast-moving swing—the unfortunate upshot of all this pushing being that it is recognized by others as pushing, and not the intended saving that Nate has in mind, in spite of his explanations. Counter explanations are subsequently offered by teachers and parents to Nate about *appropriate behavior*, the need for *respecting boundaries* and various other phrases he doesn't understand. In spite of this, Nate is undeterred in his mission, although he is for sure beginning to feel misunderstood, and decides to take his superheroing to the streets.

But in the streets Nate does not fare much better. For one thing, he is never outside the company of one or both of his parents. He is, remember, age six. If this doesn't immediately seem problematic in terms of crime prevention, try to picture the Incredible Hulk walking down the street holding hands with his mommy. It would be a hindrance, to say the least, not to mention embarrassing. Nate tries to distance himself as best he can, though, and on one occasion throws himself on top of a Rottweiler that from his vantage point appears ready to bite a small child in a stroller, only to discover too late that the Rottweiler was in fact only trying to lick the child's ice cream cone, resulting in an accidental paw punch to Nate's eye, three horrified parents, and, worse, the final retirement of the cape. Nate, depressed, takes to reading comic books in his room and napping a lot, which means he is dreaming even more, which is when a glimmer of his superpower begins to add up in his head. One afternoon Nate dreams that a certain classmate is bombarded with eggs on the playground—arguably, not so much a crime as it is bullying, and a major bummer for the classmate, nevertheless two days later, this event takes place on the playground at Nate's school, more or less exactly as he dreamt it. Nate, now forbidden to act on his impulses to save, remembers the dream but doesn't quite connect the dots until several more dream/reality occurrences take place, at which time Nate tells his parents what's been going on, at which time he is signed up for psychotherapy.

Unsurprisingly, therapy isn't terribly helpful. He's got a good enough therapist in Dr. Tuttle, but he's going under the assumption that as with most ordinary humans, Nate's dreams are clues into his psyche but nothing more than that. About a month in, Nate tells Dr. Tuttle about a particularly troubling dream in which he comes upon a young woman about to throw herself off an overpass on Lake Shore Drive. Dr. Tuttle, who always has a compassionate look on his face, again tells Nate it was just a dream, but two days later after a front-page news story about just such an event is reported, Nate returns to Dr. Tuttle, who again tells Nate the other thing he says a lot, which is that it is just a coincidence. Usually, Nate dreams of events closer to home, and his dreams aren't limited to future crimes, they're a blend of prognostication and whatever otherwise ordinary six-year-olds might dream about. Bugs and science homework and what's wrong with girls.

The following week, Nate dreams again of a potentially Nate-sized crime: a bully beating up on a scrawny kid who lives down the block. Nate doesn't suppose he could fight the bully, but he knows that he could give the kid a heads-up. Nate has begun to keep diligent notes on his dreams in a spare loose-leaf binder in his desk at home, detailing the events of each dream and then the real-life events that follow, plus dates and times of each, and has come to figure out that these incidents happen roughly within forty-eight hours of his dreams, so there's no time to waste. Nate tells his mom he's going to ride his bike, rides down to this kid's house, knocks on the door, asks to see the kid. The kid's mom is thrilled that someone's come to see her kid, Laird, who doesn't have many friends. Nate and Laird go up to Laird's room and Nate explains about the dream, and Laird, in addition to being scrawny, isn't super bright, but in this case it turns out to be to his advantage, because he believes Nate about the dream, and Nate tells him to just be sure not to walk home alone for the next few days and he'll be fine. Nate checks back with Laird every day that week to see if anything happened. Nothing did. Nate is sure his superheroing job has been done for once, though there's zero in the way of glory in this particular case.

Reporting back to Dr. Tuttle, Nate is immensely proud and excited about his first real superhero deed, and Dr. Tuttle nods, but doesn't confirm that he believes Nate. Oh, if only he had a mentor like Bob, that would be something, someone who knew, someone who could show him the ropes. He wouldn't even mind superheroing in secret—isn't that how real superheroes do it anyway?—if it weren't so problematic being six and not being able to go much of anywhere unaccompanied.

Months later, when the Pinckney-Aldersons ask their son what he wants to be for Halloween, Nate, who has silently vowed to be a practicing superhero when he grows up, in spite of Dr. Tuttle's ongoing suggestions that his dreams are coincidental, says he wants to go as Bob Brown. His parents agree to it, *As long as there's no saving.* Nate raises the possibility of cutting the front of his hair to achieve the perfect Bob Brown look, which is summarily rejected, but they do make a trip to Wigs n' Plus on Milwaukee Avenue for a wig that Nate trims very carefully in order to create just the right puff in front.

Halloween night, Bob Brown, fifteen minutes long ticked out, is at home in Albany Park with his wife—she is dressed as a Desperate Housewife (the perfect but tense redheaded one, although she briefly considered being the slutty blond one before she decided she couldn't pull it off) and Bob is wearing a Karl Rove mask, and they are handing out caramel apples, and they're not poisoned or anything, but they were on special at Aldi four weeks ago, which is to say that these apples are not at all fresh, that they are very possibly rotten, a fact Bob is completely aware of and unconcerned about. (*They're perfectly good*, Bob will say. *Apples don't go bad.*) The truth is, if all these kids got from Bob Brown was a piece of bad fruit, the worst thing likely to happen would be that they'd go home and throw up, whereas they now face the combined possibilities of vomiting and having to deal with Bob's crummy attitude and insults, and maybe even an accompanying lecture on health for any kid who dared to complain. At one point Bob Brown goes so far as to snatch a caramel apple back from the hand of a crying four-year-old dressed as Dora the Explorer whom he deems to be less than grateful, though how he judged this to be the case is uncertain.

Additionally, Bob seems to have appointed himself costume critic, as though he perceives a need for this job, as though Halloween would be more effective, as a holiday, or at least more pleasing to his aesthetic, which he seems to care a lot about, if the costumes were uniformly well considered and executed. Only very rarely does Bob declare a costume successful, and when he does, he actually uses that word, *successful*—he'll say to a kid, *Okay, now that get-up is successful*—it should be observed, always implying that the costume of someone else present is not successful, and, not unimportantly, it seems like a kid would rather hear something like *Awesome costume*, than the more dry *Successful*, or, as is more often the case, anyway, *Weak*, *Failure*, and *What the hell are you supposed to be?* Even more unfortunate is the fact that over the course of the evening Bob will proclaim four costumes to be *Offensive to my sensibilities*, three times to girls under the age of eight in various princess-type attire, once to a boy dressed as Captain America, and twice in the presence of his speechless wife. Most of the time Bob conveniently chooses to make these comments to children who do not seem to be accompanied by adults. Conceptual costumes elude Bob altogether, and several artier kids dressed as things like Joy or Office Politics or The Morning Sky leave in tears. Bob calls after one kid's father, *If your goal is for your kid to be an outcast, kudos. Kudos on being a total dick,* the father yells back, and Mrs. Brown, slightly tipsy from the cognac she started sipping straight out of the bottle after Bob's first few insults of the night, cannot suppress a giggle.

Of course, there are more than a few questions about Nate's costume. Several people guess that he's a Munchkin. Others guess from the colors and the cape that he's a Best Buy salesman, which would be a good guess if any kid would ever go out for Halloween dressed as a Best Buy salesman in a cape. (*It says* BB *on the back*, says a snarky fourteen-year-old in an oversized trench coat who either isn't in costume or is dressed like an old-time private eye. *Aren't you a little old for this*, asks Mrs. Pinckney-Alderson, in a fakey-sweet tone, to which the trench-coat kid says, *Aren't you a little old?*) Eventually, Nate's mom loses count of how many times during the night her son tells people he's Bob Brown, the superhero, and she seems grateful that Nate does not seem frustrated by the experience. By complete coincidence, Nate ends up at the real Bob Brown's house, though Bob Brown himself does not recognize Nate's homage, and because he's wearing the creepy Karl Rove mask, he himself is unrecognizable to Nate. But Bob's wife knows, or thinks she does, and she giggles and bends down to whisper in Nate's ear that she thinks his costume is *very authentic*, which of course makes his night even though he simultaneously receives a *That looks nothing like Superman!* from his adult counterpart. Nate is about to explain to Bob Brown that he is not in fact Superman, but before he has a chance to finish, his mother, eager to avoid any further abuse from the man in the Karl Rove mask, drags her son off to the next house.

Over the course of the night, very few people get it really, even after Nate's repeated explanations, but most try to pretend they do, and he stands out, in his little middle-aged-man outfit, among the ghosts, goblins, Teletubbies, and SpongeBobs (a Bob Nate is decidedly uninterested in), yet he seems neither to know or care. Nate seems very focused on explaining to anyone who will listen that he is dressed as a man who saves a baby.

That night, Nate dreams of the man in the Karl Rove mask. It is an absolutely terrible, frightening dream that wakes him up and sends him down the hall crying to his parents. The man in the Karl Rove mask is being brutally beaten by a group of teenagers in the parking lot of his school. After the kids leave, it seems as though the man in the Karl Rove mask may not make it.

When the news of what happened to Bob Brown breaks, Mrs. Pinckney-Alderson shakes her head. Nate comes downstairs in his pajamas and asks his mother if there's been any story in the news about the man in the mask, and even with this clue, she doesn't connect the dots; the Karl Rove mask of Nate's dream has sufficiently obscured his identity for all concerned.

Bob's condition is initially dire, though he will eventually make a full recovery. A small fund-raiser held by the school will help defray some of his rehab costs that weren't covered by his insurance, and for about a second, maybe a portion of a second, Bob Brown will allow himself to fully feel the goodness of humanity, though it's an unbearably uncomfortable portion of a second, and in subsequent seconds he will return to dismissing this kindness as a rare, isolated incident.

Nate's commitment to superheroing will remain unceasing for the next few years until he hits seventh grade and discovers that there's not that much wrong with girls at all, that actually there's a lot right with them, or at least the one named Olivia in the homeroom next to his. Olivia wears jeans with holes in the knees and he can't pinpoint it exactly but those knees have more or less altered the world as he knows it. Olivia, whom he sees only in passing in the hallway, has no real idea of his existence at least insofar as he might have a name, but it almost doesn't matter. Slowly all things Olivia begin to supercede all things saving, and though he will fare no better with Olivia than with the superheroing, one day both will be in the distance.

Turf

The story you are about to hear is made up and the reason it's made up is because we don't know the half of it. But just in case it seems familiar, rest assured that names, places, and details are made up too. This story takes place in the large Midwestern city of Hicago, which as you are surely aware, does not even exist, much of it not existing at a dog park very close to the intersection of Hackhawk and Heaver, which is also made up. So there should be no concern, we think, about anyone's feelings getting hurt, or any misunderstandings or what have you.

The two main characters here are the dog walker Hulie and the dog owner Helizabeth.

Hulie, we're pretty sure, has lived on that block her whole life. She's maybe twenty-six. Twenty-six years ago that block was rough. Ten years ago that block was rough. Now there are some condos, but sometimes in the mornings we'll see so much shattered glass by the curb, we wonder about the window-smashing spree the night before, who around here thinks that's a good time. We don't have suspicions, but we think Hulie might.

Helizabeth has lived on Heaver Street for about five years now. More is known, factually, about Helizabeth than Hulie because Helizabeth is a local author and you can Google her just like she does. Hulie doesn't even go online, we'd say. So anyway Helizabeth and her then-boyfriend-now-husband Hen moved in there together, got married a few months later in the backyard. Last year, having postponed making the baby decision for a while, Helizabeth and Hen decided it was time to get a dog, and a sweet stray found its way to them through a friend at the Hatahoula Rescue, and Helizabeth and Hen brought home their new baby, a sickly fifty-pound ten-month-old with a soft gray coat covered with the trademark Hatahoula purple, pink, and white markings. They named him Herky.

Initially, Herky was a mellow dog, awkward in social settings; no way was he alpha, he wasn't even beta, more like mu or nu or omicron. At the dog park, Herky would make efforts to play, wagging his butt and bouncing around in that puppy way, but inevitably, after annoying one of the alphas with his eager doggy dorkiness, he'd end up pushed into a corner. He was not one of the cool kids.

But over the year, Herky gained a few pounds along with some confidence, and although he still never became alpha, he for sure moved up to maybe around theta. He still isn't much interested in bossing anyone around, and will never start a fight, but if you do, he will defend himself.

What we actually know about Hulie: She has a Great Hane named Hurphy. Around noon every day, she arrives at the dog park with a minivan full of barking dogs, stays there for a couple of hours. Every so often, she'll throw a well-chewed ball for them, but calling this game *fetch* would be a stretch because it tends to be a long time between throws, and we've never one time witnessed her showing affection to a dog. Not one time. She appears to know a lot of folks in the immediate vicinity, and will frequently engage in lengthy conversation with them. Words and phrases we overhear in these conversations regularly include *terrible*, *I'm not*, and *I never.* Hulie doesn't smile much in these conversations, or ever. Hulie yells at her dogs a lot and we've also seen her hit them. The police have come around to see her, but not because of that. What Hulie does, bringing the dogs to the park, isn't really legal, but because she seems to know so many folks, it seems that someone in the hood is looking out for her. There's an ex-congressman on the block (famously corrupt), and we've seen them chatting.

What we think we know about Hulie: Her boyfriend, Hoger, lives downstairs from her. It's possible that they live together, but probably not. Our best guess is that they met in the laundry room. Her apartment is sparsely decorated, if the word *decorated* is even appropriate. She'd like it to be a little nicer, but just doesn't know how to go about it, doesn't really have the time. There are a couple of pictures hung in odd locations, too high or low, no doubt on nails that were already in the walls. There's a spider plant in a macramé hanger by the window, but lately it doesn't look so good. Sometimes at Walgreens she'll pick up a scented Glade candle. Her sofa is a futon in a frame; on it is an earth-toned afghan she thinks her grandmother crocheted, but that isn't true. That was a story her mother told her. No one knows who made it. Hulie doesn't cook much, will get a roasted chicken or a salad at the Jewel, maybe something frozen from Aldi, but that's a little too far down Hilwaukee and she's not over that way too much and plus it smells bad. Once a year her boyfriend will take her to some fancy sushi place like Haponais, because he heard celebrities go there. But she won't really be impressed, and she won't really like it. She will order something cooked.

Her bedroom is more or less the same. She sleeps on a mattress on the floor and there's a large pile of laundry in the corner. Hurphy isn't allowed to sleep in the bed, but since her bed is close to the floor, Hurphy sleeps right next to her on the nights when Hoger isn't over. When Hoger is over Hurphy sleeps in the living room because Hoger doesn't like the dog watching them fuck. Hoger's words.

In her bathroom, Hulie's bikini panties are strewn about, the kind that have words on the butt in big letters, words like SEXY or HOTT. This is about as girly as she gets, really she's kind of a tomboy, but she uses Suave Juicy Green Apple Shampoo, there's a curling iron on the sink, and on New Year's Eve Helizabeth saw her walking Hurphy in a long black jersey gown under her fleece jacket. She may have also been wearing blush.

When she's not hanging out with Hoger, once in a while she'll watch those home-improvement shows where people come in and fix up a room for under a thousand dollars, and thinks how nice it would be to have someone do that for her. The last book she read was *Men Are from Mars, Women Are from Venus*, which her sister had sent her from Arizona (she'd gotten the fuck out of the neighborhood and all the way out of the state as soon as she graduated high school), but Hulie didn't finish it because it was a bunch of horseshit she already knew anyhow and she wasn't likely to take her sister's advice on romance seeing as how she was married to a blazing asshole. Hulie's sister is twelve years older, but they were never very close even in that almost-parent-sisterly kind of way. Hulie does not have a group of girlfriends, does not have a girlfriend, has not had a girlfriend since her childhood friend Hennifer totally made out with her boyfriend Hichie right in front of her face at her own thirteenth birthday party. Hennifer had tried to point out that in kissing games you kiss, but Hulie wasn't having it. Mostly, in her spare time, Hulie does sudoku or hangs around out front with whoever's playing cornhole.

So Hulie dates Hoger, and she works with dogs but she doesn't smile. How does someone work with dogs and not smile, like, constantly? We wonder if somebody hit her. If we weren't so sure she's been on this block since forever, we'd wonder if she was one of those foster kids you hear about who gets moved sixteen times and hit in fifteen of them. We wonder if someone hit her somewhere along the line because we can't come up with any other reason why someone who works with dogs would just never smile. We hope it wasn't Hoger, but we could believe it. Or maybe in ninth grade she was on color guard and kind of liked it and would defend it as totally being a sport but skipped it one afternoon to meet a cute druggy boy behind the physical plant and never went back because he said it was way lame and she spent the next two years alternating between doing it with him in his garage and getting hit by him if she wasn't in the mood or if she had her period. Probably, she wanted to be something else, once.

What little we know about Hoger: Hoger has a great head of hair but he seems to favor an old-school heavy Brylcreem look, slicked straight back, very Gordon Gekko. He wears a suit to work (maybe at the Hoard of Trade?), some designer suit that he paid a thousand dollars for so he can tell people it's Hugo Boss except after he got it off the rack he never took it to get tailored and so it doesn't fit quite right. Okay, I guess we don't know that for sure but that's what it looks like. We do know that he has a Hottweiler named Hex and that when he brings Hex to the dog park he stays for about the length of a smoke or until Hex makes, Hoger's word, whichever comes first. We suspect Hoger isn't one to really decorate either, but we are completely sure he has that framed poster of naked Nastassja Kinski with the snake. Never mind that it's before his era. He saw it on sale at a dollar store for five dollars and ninety-nine cents and his mind was blown. Hulie doesn't care for it one bit, but Hoger won't budge. He tells her when she poses naked with a snake he'll take it down. She tells him he can fuck Nastassja Kinski until that day and he says, You think I couldn't hit that? And she says, Whatever, she's like fifty now anyways, go ahead.

Helizabeth and Hen's apartment is a rental and it's big and old and perpetually dusty but it's filled with books and art; Hen is an artist. Helizabeth makes books. They don't have tons of money or anything, but they have some nice pieces of furniture and Helizabeth makes curtains and pillows and it feels like a home. Hen built a bed for Herky. They too have a laundry pile, but Helizabeth tries her best to make sure it stays in the closet. They drink loose tea and grind their coffee and are working on going organic and weaning off sugar, if it weren't for the problem of things like Hunky Monkey ice cream being so good. They shop mostly at Trader Ho's but if they have a little extra cash some week they'll splurge at Hole Foods.

One morning, Helizabeth took Herky out for his morning walk—Hen is on mornings most days, but it was a holiday and those are usually Helizabeth's. Herky and Helizabeth were playing fetch when Hulie came in with Hurphy and Hex and another dog. Helizabeth and Hulie had a brief conversation but perhaps the longest they'd ever had. Something like Hey. Hey. Dust from the construction is terrible, huh? Awful, yeah. I cleaned up a ton of their garbage too. They never clean it up. I'm always doing that. Yeah, I had to tell a guy to put his beer bottles in the trash. What guy? I dunno, some guy that told me he lives right over here. I know that guy, he doesn't live there. I heard he got his girlfriend pregnant and she doesn't want anything to do with him so he comes out here to drink. Oh. I know, can you believe it? I've told him so many times . . . Are you dog sitting this weekend? Story of my life. Hulie nods and rolls her eyes like it's a perpetual drag. Still, Helizabeth, we guess, feels bad for judging Hulie so harshly because Hulie's sadness is so obvious, and sees a small window where maybe they'll have a conversation in the positive someday, maybe chat about *Grey's Anatomy* or Britney Spears or something.

Something else that is known by all parties: Hex is a ball hog. You pretty much can't have Hex and a ball in the park together if you're interested in holding on to that ball. If Hex gets the ball, the ball belongs to Hex. Otherwise, Hex is pretty agreeable as dogs go. Usually, Helizabeth will take the ball away from Herky when Hex comes in but in this case waited until it was too late, and an incident occurred.

There are differences of opinion about the specifics of this incident, but the result was that Herky, no longer a shy, sickly puppy, emboldened by his health and new robustness, decided not to allow the taking of the ball, and a brief dogfight occurred. Helizabeth and Hulie broke the fight up quickly, but not before Hex left with a cut on his lip and Herky left with a small but deep gash in his side.

Helizabeth's solution to this problem was to avoid the dog park around lunchtime.

A couple of weeks went by and Helizabeth was at the park with Herky around 11 a.m. when Hulie was leaving to pick up her dogs. What we could make of it: Hulie came over and tried to start a conversation about it. Something like, Listen, I'm hearing that you're going around saying Hex attacked your dog and that's not what happened. Helizabeth said something like Where did you hear that? and Hulie said Dog park gossip, and Helizabeth said Well I never said *attacked*, I said *bit*, and Hulie said But why were you even talking about it and Helizabeth said Look at that gash, people were asking, even the vet was like Whoa, what happened here? and Hulie said You didn't have to take him to the vet, and Helizabeth said What? And Hulie said Did he get stitches? And Helizabeth said No and Hulie said Then you didn't need to go to the vet and Helizabeth, getting to that point in the argument where you start defending yourself by making lists, said Okay, (a) We didn't know if he needed stitches or not, and (b) Who are you to tell me whether I should take my dog to the vet, and Hulie said I see it all the time, dogs get cut up, it's no big deal, Helizabeth said Okay, whatever, this has nothing to do with anything, and Hulie said Anyways I just didn't like what I heard, and Helizabeth said, Well I told you the truth, and Hulie said But that's not what I heard what I heard was *attacked*, and this *attacked*-versus-*bit* thing went around a few more times and Helizabeth said Look, I can't make you believe me and then at this point there was a rehashing of the incident, Hulie said that Herky started it and Helizabeth said No, Herky growled as if to warn Hex off, and then Hex went after Herky, and Hulie said That's not true because you had your back turned, you don't even know, and Helizabeth at this point was starting to lose it, and we've never seen her like this before, although it's not unbelievable, we imagine her as the sort of person who can remain calm through quite a number of circumstances way worse than a disagreement at the dog park but then will reach a point where she begins to lose it, and this was that point, and Helizabeth raised up her arms dramatically and said Are you joking me? I was facing you, we were talking, and the dogs were between us and Hulie said Well I don't know and Helizabeth said Well I know! I know! and Hulie also said A lot of people are saying they don't want to come in here when Herky's here, and Helizabeth said WHAT, WHAT, who, who are these "a lot of people," and Hulie named a dog and Helizabeth said Herky and that dog were friends until he started a fight with Herky, and his mom knows that, and Hulie said Well I'm just telling you what I hear, that a lot of people are afraid of Herky and Helizabeth said Who else? And Hulie, whose unaffected demeanor only served to further raise Helizabeth's hackles, named this other dog and Helizabeth said That is the most ill-mannered dog whose parents have no control over him whatsoever, and he harasses Herky, not the other way around and those people know it too. Everyone leaves the park when that dog comes in. And Hulie said Well I'm just telling you what I hear and Helizabeth said Who else? and Hulie said Well that's all I know and Helizabeth said Well that's two dogs which isn't a lot especially since it's them and not Herky so I don't see how that's a lot, actually I don't see how that's any, especially considering I heard your boyfriend bragged about Hex eating a puppy for lunch. Which at that moment was arguably neither here nor there, we had the impression that this was a point Helizabeth might have used more effectively at a different point in her argument. Hulie told her If he did say that she was sure it was a joke and Helizabeth said that that wasn't the impression she had and Hulie said Well I don't know alls I know is there's a lot of gossip and I don't want anyone to feel uncomfortable or like whoever wants to come here can't come here. And at this point Helizabeth appeared to be at a loss for words but finally said Well, I feel like it's understood that this is your corner, and Hulie said Well I'm sorry if I gave you that impression, did I give you that impression? and Helizabeth said I don't know if you gave it to me but that's the impression I have and Hulie said Well I'm sorry about that, I don't want to give that impression and Helizabeth shrugged like she thought Hulie really did want to give that impression and said Well it's just a little intimidating and Hulie said Well that's too bad, like she meant it, like she was genuinely implying that it was too bad that Helizabeth felt too intimidated to come back to the park but that she'd probably get over it fast enough even though just that holiday morning, before the incident, our guess is that Hulie had started to turn a corner on Helizabeth, thinking maybe she wasn't so bad. It seemed to us like in that moment they both knew the other wasn't so bad but that they'd had their shot and it was over. We also speculate that Hulie, still stung by the junior high make-out debacle with Hennifer, was less surprised than mildly disappointed. This may seem like all of it except in reality it went on for nearly an hour and also it was about seventeen degrees outside at the time.

What was learned? Immediately after the incident, Helizabeth thought it was a strong indicator that it was time to leave Hicago or at least to move off the block.

We speculate that Helizabeth and Hulie both had long conversations with their significant others, maybe more than one, and that Hoger and Hen both stood by their women, and that requests were put in by both women that this incident not be mentioned again unless they were prepared for an argument, rational or otherwise. All we know for sure is that Helizabeth doesn't go to the park at noon anymore and Hulie still doesn't smile.

There's a lady on the block, a little old lady in a head scarf, who every day gives bread to the birds and the cats and dogs. This seems to be her genuine joy and we don't want to take this away from her. We call her the bread lady and she always smiles, always. But she doesn't know anything for sure either.

Video

We did not exist before now. We are young and nameless and our skin is unblemished and our hair is just like this and we keep our faces blank, always. There's a boy who likes me; though his face is blank and he does not speak, I can tell because he is facing in my direction. Some of us wear old man glasses, though no one is old here and we do not read. We are thin with the effortless slimness that comes with youth. Our shirts are flannel and our knitted caps defy gravity. They say my hair is cut like Sharon Tate's, but I don't know who that is. I don't know who anyone is. I run in slow motion through the woods. It's very moody and pretty when I do this. See how my hair swings behind me? The boy who likes me follows.

We drive around Los Angeles at night, these girls and me, two in the front and two in the back of a vintage convertible. It doesn't matter what kind. I wouldn't know. One girl might be Asian, I'm not sure. We look at everything but each other. Another girl has hair that is short on one side and long on the other, she could be gay, and the third girl has a nose ring, but we are all supposed to be the same. I wave my hand in the air below the palm trees like they tell me. My hand is pretty. Our hair blows in the wind, in slow motion. Whatever we do, we do it in slow motion. We turn our heads to look at the passing landscape in slow motion. Everything looks best in slow motion. A couple fighting, a drunk girl stumbling, two old ladies with fancy hats go by in slow motion. It's like a beautiful dream. A homeless man with a train of grocery carts turns to look at us in slow motion. He sees our beauty and in him seeing our beauty we see it in him.

There is one boy who looks bad. He wears a new old man's hat. His face is blank too, but in a bad way. He's gone soon enough though.

The boy and I are in the woods again. I keep running, but now I have on a bunny mask, which makes me mysterious but also playful. I can tell the boy still likes me because now we are hugging. We never speak and our faces remain blank, but we convey things with our facial stillness and our perfect hair.

Some boys in tight pants and flat sneakers swerve by on skateboards. Then they're gone.

The bunny mask is gone now. The boy puts a cap on me but it's itchy, and I think it looks dumb there on the back of my head doing nothing. My hair is so pretty. I'm not cold. I don't need a hat. You don't get a say, they say. This is what the young people wear. This is how the boy shows that he cares. If he really cared, he would ask if I was cold. He would ask if I liked the hat.

Your face is not blank enough now, they say. It needs to be more blank. You're falling in love. Think about nothing. That doesn't make any sense, I tell them. Well, then think about something that makes you feel blank, they say. Blank isn't a feeling, I say.

The boy and I begin to walk out of sight into the woods, holding hands. It's supposed to be the end but I decide to improvise. I drop the boy's hand and run a little bit and then I run backward a few paces and smile. You're asking for trouble! they yell. You have no idea what's out there! I shrug, big. I shrug big and make a big shrug face and I head for what's out there.

Wind

On the last day of her life, my grandmother woke up, went into the bathroom to brush her teeth, and looked into the mirror to discover that she was bald. *Oh!* she said. *That's a fright. This won't do at all.* My grandmother took great pride in her appearance, and she'd had her soft white curls washed and set every Friday for the last forty years. Once a month she'd get a permanent. One time when I was about seven she took me with her to the beauty parlor to get ready for Easter Sunday. She let me get a manicure while she sat with her rods in. *Pale pink only, though*, she'd instructed when I picked up a sparkly purple. *That won't do.* While we were both drying, she told me of a trip she once took to New York City. *A marvel*, she'd said.

Oh! my grandmother said again, and feeling herself wobbling, she sat down on the edge of the tub. At the hospital, she remarked that she'd felt grateful she'd remembered to close the bathroom window the night before, because that morning she felt as though a strong breeze could have blown her right over.

I've lost my hair, she told the doctors and nurses. Her baldness was very clearly her only concern. They explained that she had a condition, that it wasn't uncommon, that they were going to run some tests but that they expected to release her before the end of the day. *Yes, but what shall I do about my hair?* she asked. The suggestion of a wig was not the right answer.

One of the nurses practiced acupuncture on the side. She explained to me and my dad that this kind of hair loss is a wind condition. *A very strong wind!* my grandmother said. We laughed. She died before the end of the day. *Old age,* the doctor said, *maybe a stroke. Hard to know.*

When we went to her house to choose an outfit for her funeral, I saw my grandmother's hair. It was fanned out in her head shape on her pale pink pillowcase, a halo, an abstract painting, and it was no longer curled, but pin straight. I thought of what the nurse had said about the wind thing. I imagined it blowing through the container of her this way, strong enough to push out her hair at the root. I imagined it picking her up and carrying her off on a spectacular aerial tour of the world that would last exactly long enough for her hair to grow back, gently setting her back down in the beauty parlor, where she'd get a wash and set and tell her girl about her marvelous trip.

We Collect Things

Our deal is we collect things. The only requirement for membership is a collection of one thousand things. More is fine. More is better. Our preference is for collections of just one type of thing, but we are not exclusive in this way. Our members are not just one thing, why should our collections be?

Some of us collect the usual: stamps, coins, rocks, toys, baseball cards, lunch boxes, salt and pepper shakers, snow globes, thimbles, spoons, paperweights, matchbooks, hot sauces, license plates, bells, whistles, Barbies, butterflies, insects, wind-up toys, instruments, vintage purses, potato mashers, cameras, teapots, royal commemorative mugs (royal everything), action figures, figurines (ceramic, vinyl, historic, pack animals only), bobbleheads, erasers, pencils, pens (fountain, float), pennies (wheat, smashed), buttons (political, notions, and otherwise), watches (pocket, wrist), magazines (*Life*, *Look*, *TV Guide*, *MAD*), Jesus things, Elvis things, presidential busts (small, large), Mold-A-Ramas, autographs, comic books, rocks, robots, refrigerator magnets, snuff boxes, shot glasses, typewriters, sewing machines, PEZ dispensers, marbles, Jew's harps, velvet paintings, miniature anything and everything, transit memorabilia, bottles shaped like things, serving dishes shaped like the food you serve them in, owls, cows, anything with an owl or a cow (or a cow print) on it.

Some of us get super specific: vintage Ouija board planchettes pre-1950, velvet dog paintings, postcards postmarked from a certain state, vintage sheet music printed only in a certain state, many and various specific items relating to a certain state, loose parts to the game of Operation (no tweezers), square-shaped moist towelettes, green fishing lures, turquoise vintage hair dryers, blue things (and red things and pink things and every color things but blue is the biggest of the color things), pretty much anything you can think of in only a certain shape or color, mini-cacti all propagated from a single mini-cactus, mini–troll dolls wearing eyeglasses and handmade dresses, mini–teddy bears wearing crew neck sweaters, bird nests found in Eastern Seaboard states, white marble doorknobs, five-sided shards of pottery, Polaroids of strangers at parties with writing on the bottom, dried flowers that came from someone's wedding, Eiffel Towers/Empire State Buildings/Leaning Towers of Pisa/Great Pyramids and Sphinxes under six inches tall, burnt matches (unbroken), mix tapes that include "I Never Knew Love Like This Before" by Stephanie Mills (far fewer than a thousand in this collection, but her devotion to this song touched us), handwritten pink receipts for office supplies, vintage round fluorescent kitchen lightbulbs, sneakers that once hung on electrical wires in the Bronx.

Some of us collect things that you can get for free: the little plastic tags that come on the end of your bread (the collectors call these bread tags, but for our purposes we won't assume you know that names even exist for half of the things we collect), grocery lists left behind in shopping carts, ticket stubs, fabric scraps, takeout menus, fortune cookie fortunes, business cards, feathers, rocks shaped like hearts, rocks shaped like things, shells, beach glass, driftwood, plastic items found on the beach (combs are big), ketchup packets, salt packets, sweetener packets (packets are big), ticket stubs, paint chips, pencils that have been used and sharpened down to where they can no longer be sharpened. Lids. Just lids. Plastic, metal, glass, just lids.

There are things that people collect that a lot of people collect that are more like just things you have a lot of, like books and records. So we ask that book and record collectors who wish to join think more specifically. First editions. Autographed books. Phone books. Miniature books. Books with *love* in the title. Books with any same word in the title. Books with fancy endpapers. *Moby-Dick* that has someone else's notes and underlines inside. Cylindrical records. Record adapters. Grateful Dead concert bootlegs (tapes only). Springsteen concert bootlegs (tapes only, recorded in New Jersey only). Records or recordings made by or somehow involving Robert Pollard.

Basically, if a thing exists, someone out there has a collection of it.

We hope you will understand if your collection was not noted here. There is simply not the space here for a comprehensive list. Should you be interested, please see Dave in Membership.

Regarding displays: It really depends on what you collect. Small things can be displayed on shelves. Shelves can be customized. Flat things can be displayed in files and drawers, but we require easy access and complete cataloguing. Larger collections may require larger wall space or larger homes, but there are all kinds of creative ways to display things and we love visiting each other's homes both to see collections and for inspiration. Bigger things require bigger places in which to display them, so if you have it in your mind to build a collection of something like farming machinery, vintage campers, or automobiles, we advise caution. That such collections are prohibitively costly does not seem to prohibit some of us, and that is but one pitfall of your large-item collecting.

You may already know that there are entire conventions dedicated to some of these collections, Legos, Hummels, Disney, comic books, salt and pepper shakers, it goes on. We always ask if you're sure that isn't what you'd prefer, though we feel we offer a broader experience. But it's not either/or.

We are not in the collectible business. We do not sell our items, unless under duress. We do encourage trades.

As we grew, we have had occasion to have some meetings.

We held a meeting once, because some people tried to join with collections that were frankly kind of disgusting. There was a lengthy discussion about what was disgusting and what wasn't and how do we determine that. Finally we voted. We voted on voting when any new members joined, even if their collections were very obviously not disgusting, like Hello Kitty collections or whatever. There was one anti-HK argument based on the disgustingness of capitalism, but these types are not our kind, plus if you put a Hello Kitty in someone's sight line, you could call us annoying, but most likely she will have made our point for us. Take your capitalism beefs to the Birkin bag collectors, who think they're too good for us. We ruled out a few things. People collect animals. We decided: No live things, no dead things. No to bodily fluids. (You can take that from there.) Taxidermy was a close vote, but it was in. Haunted dolls were another close vote, though we voted them in because most of us didn't really believe in ghosts. Nazi or KKK memorabilia or anything like it was a no-way, no-how. Mammies came up for discussion again and again; it's hard to find a way to acknowledge our history in a sensitive way, so we try to clarify motives. Let's just say that if you're Caucasian and you've got a collection of mammy dolls, it is not going to suffice for you to proclaim yourself a historian, and if you call us reverse racists, we will show you to the door. Yes, this is sometimes dodgy, but keep in mind that we are not trying to tell you not to collect these things, simply that this invites a type of controversy we are not interested in dealing with. There are other groups for you with their doors wide open. The real trouble comes in when we come upon a collection that is broad enough to be able to include one or two of these items. It should go without saying that people are constantly adding to their collections (very little culling ever occurs, though we have great admiration for those collectors who are able to do so), and that there are sometimes items about which we are unaware. We aim for an atmosphere of trust, but you know how that sometimes goes.

We had big discussions about pornography and ultimately voted against all of it, hoping to be clear that it didn't mean we were against porn altogether. Mainly, we feared there were too many unknowns regarding production, especially with child porn sneaking in there, and our only member who was into porn more than casually was reluctant to be assigned to the task of investigating. Guns and ammo were voted in by an extremely narrow margin. We are very, very careful with guns and ammo collectors. There are guidelines and restrictions that we don't have time to outline here, but the big one is that you may collect one or the other but not both. We feel strongly that keeping these two things separate solves a lot of potential problems and addresses many fears. Obviously, there are those guns and ammo enthusiasts who can no more separate these two things than they could themselves separate H_2 from O and are affronted if we suggest they try. So if you are a collector of guns or ammo, we usually suggest other groups first. But if you feel you're a collector before you're a guns or ammo person, Bunny in Restrictions and Checks will see you now. Be prepared to wait. Has it been pointed out to us that these two choices, when considered together, indicate that we are anti-sex and pro-violence? Yes. Yes, it has. Here we invite you to visit with our numerous collectors of various kinds of sex toys, blow-up dolls, and Frederick's of Hollywood cutout lingerie; Sandy Q's delightful collection of pink dildos is highly recommended, and we have countless collections relating to the Summer of Love, Woodstock, and every imaginable type of peace sign as well. Ulla's collection of Gandhi memorabilia has caught the attention of several notable historians. Just sayin'.

People collect grudges. Do you have a thousand grudges? We asked. Some of them did. Did we want people with a thousand grudges? Did we want to send them away with a thousand and one? What about slights? Could we accommodate a thousand slights? Would the weight of a thousand slights add up to a grudge? People collect ideas. Were we to exclude these people? It didn't feel like what a lot of us were about. How do you display an idea? Display was everything to us. Surely there was another group for people with ideas. We weren't against ideas. They just weren't our thing. Plus how could we decide what ideas were legitimate to collect and what weren't? We argued among ourselves about this. Violence was clearly a bad idea. We agreed on that. If you collected violent ideas, we would have to say no, and gently suggest getting help. Political ideas? *No, thank you*. On this we agreed as well. We didn't care if your political ideas aligned with ours, and we certainly welcomed collections of political memorabilia across party lines. But these are things that *represent* ideas, and there is a distinction. Abstract ideas? Too abstract, can't decide, probably not. Do you realize how many obviously bad ideas some people collect? Some of these idea people were certain we were the right group for them. If you had good ideas for products or things that would make the world a better place, okay then. If you had good ideas for art projects but you weren't an artist, you were in. (On both of these, we were pleased with ourselves for providing options for people who knew how to develop ideas but didn't actually have any.) We decided that when it came to ideas, we would vote. Could you find a way to display your ideas, a way that itself was not abstract? Could your idea be framed, pinned, or shelved? (This led to further discussion: one guy collected shelved ideas. We told him if he could literally shelve his shelved ideas, he was good to go.) We let those people in. Clichés? One of our own tried to make his case against clichés by saying he didn't want to rock the boat but that he felt we should avoid clichés like the plague. Adages and aphorisms? Several adage collectors were not fond of aphorists, who they believed were not as rooted in the tradition of proverb and therefore less worthy. But we voted them all in, and let maxims in as well. Metaphors? Similes? There were some among us (English teachers, mostly) who squabbled about the need for both metaphors and similes, and on a related note, one left us in a huff altogether over the suggestion that anything could ever truly be like anything else (her argument that we were all as unique as snowflakes was perhaps ill-considered), but to these we voted yes. If you can display them, sure. This isn't about need.

We came upon a real problem. We're not above gossip, and it went around that there was a Nazi button in one of the button collections. There were hundreds of button collectors. Bunny from Restrictions and Checks worked overtime to locate it. Gerry made his case that it was not a collection of Nazi memorabilia, that he was not a Nazi, did not support Nazis in any way, that he rather took offense to the suggestion that he did, that this was a historic button like all his buttons. As we noted, items are added or slip in on occasion. Gerry threatened a think piece. We threatened response pieces. We are not afraid of a think piece. (Been there.) We told him it was him or the button. We are not sure we did the right thing. Gerry's think piece did not make us look worse than he did, but Charlene went ahead with her response piece, to which Gerry responded, all of which was followed by a Twitter war, #teamGerry and #teamCharlene, as well as numerous response pieces to the whole affair in some high-profile outlets. Eventually, we were forced to run interference with a publicist, which was costly. We might have done better to let the whole thing blow over after Gerry opened his big trap. But as Charlene pointed out, our arguments were essentially the same: both sides were accusing the other of exclusivity, and it may well be that we all were, but this is the kind of thing that sometimes gets the better of us. Our numbers dwindled for a time in the wake of The Great Think/Response Debacle.

We strongly suggest making provisions in your wills and discussing them with your loved ones in advance. We have seen what happens when we don't. As often as not, our relatives have strongly negative feelings about our things. If your son or daughter suggests to you that they will burn your beloved Beanie Babies in a bonfire on the beach the moment you meet your maker, believe them. Bonfires are real. One of our fellows, while in hospice, was made aware of a bonfire of his vast collection of vintage paper popcorn buckets, and upon seeing photos, nearly died right then. (This was a particularly cruel incident, one we've come to think of as our driver's ed movie, the bad accident we share to alarm you into action if we feel you are unconvinced.) Please note, however, that when planned for and under controlled circumstances, a bonfire can provide a beautiful sendoff for the right kind of collection and can be part of a moving and necessary ceremony for those left behind. Most family members could not accommodate a fraction of what they might inherit even if they were interested; most others simply take a few cherished items to remember their loved one by, and donate the rest. The hard truth is that many of our close friends and relatives will not want any part of our collections; this information usually comes to us unsolicited, well before the subject of inheritance is ever raised, and it has been proven, disastrously so, that we ourselves cannot absorb other collections. Goodwill and the like are invariably forced to trash most of what is donated, collection-wise. We'll let you sit with that for a minute. But there are more options than it may seem. One among us has requested in writing that upon her death, her collection of rocks be thrown into Lake Michigan. We find this to be a beautiful thing to imagine, family and friends on a boat or on the shore, returning the stones of their loved ones to the world in this way. (Bird nests as well, though they tend to float, so we suggest setting them down gently on the water's edge and watching them drift away.) Please note this as an option for you to consider if you are a collector of such items from nature—rocks, sea glass, shells. For obvious reasons, we urge you to refrain from throwing anything else into the sea. And we urge you to be realistic. We are aware of how we are often seen by noncollectors. We suggest researching museums, and archives, as well as talking with other collectors younger than you who might be interested. We can also refer you to counselors who specialize in talking you through your fears about such things.

The media often takes an interest in us. We're not opposed to this. Aside from the Gerry fiasco, which did get some coverage, they tend to be the folksy, charming little feel-good stories at the end of the nightly or local news. *Oh, look at these cute people with their hobbies*. Sometimes, we get asked about how we can afford our collections, why we don't spend our money in "better" ways. *So judgy*, some of us say. *We work*, others of us say. Most of us aren't wealthy. We just know what we like. We have been asked what the difference between collecting and hoarding is. We know it's sometimes a fine line, sometimes not. There are those among us who have bought properties to store and display their collections. We ask you to consider if your health is affected. Do you want people to visit? We do like to visit. Those are questions we ask any new member. We ask about health, visits, displays. If the answers are right, we send people out. We have guidelines, but we're not the hoarder police. We care. We talk to family members. We have seen people cross the line. We try to tell ourselves it could not happen to us, but we don't like to think about it. One of our dearest was killed when an unsecured bookcase toppled onto her and pinned her beneath her lifetime of journals. (Then near eighty, Bernice had filled several hundred volumes and of course she also collected blank ones for future use, though it would have taken her several more lifetimes to fill the ones in the future-use category.) This was a grim discovery, as evidence suggested that she died not of injuries sustained but of starvation, and when some among us began reading her deadly oeuvre, ugly revelations came to light suggesting our dear friend had not thought quite so dearly of us in return. We had more than a few discussions of ethics after this, but the bigger upshot was that some of us became worried that Bernice wasn't the only one of us with so much hidden ill will. This was less due to specific incidents or names cited in Bernice's texts than it was the strength of her conviction that there was widespread malice and envy among our members. Accusations emerged, several members fell away, and longtime friendships broke apart over what was mostly just paranoia. We have since implemented a detailed list of suggested guidelines for good citizenship and securing your collections, but we simply can't monitor people, and we still rely greatly on your good judgment. We do call the authorities, sometimes. We don't like to.

We get asked where it ends. It doesn't, we say. It ends when we run out of shelving. Usually we just make more shelving. We're prepared to build into the sky, if necessary.

Today in Post-Apocalyptic Problems

A couple years later.

It was the day after we'd put our old dog down that I opened the front door to discover a baby in a bucket on our doorstep. Remember how hard it used to be to have to take a beloved pet to the vet to put her to sleep? Now you had to do it yourself. A different way. A way I'd rather not talk about.

These are the chances you take when you make a choice to open your door these days. Some days you can almost forget that it's different now; other days you've just killed your own dog and there's a baby in a paint bucket on your front porch. Seriously like out of some '40s movie, except it's neither funny nor cute. This baby did not look well. He looked too sickly to cry even.

So I brought the baby inside and I said, *Honey, our new problem is here*, which is a running joke now, and he said, cheerfully,

Yeah? What is it today? and I said, *Today in Post-Apocalyptic Problems is proud to present: It's a baby*, and he said, *A baby what?* which was when I walked into the living room with the bucket baby. *Congratulations*, I said. *It's a boy.* We both smiled, but this was something else. This would have been something else ten years ago, when Huggies still existed. But now, this was something else something else. This was: I am already very tired, I was born tired, and now I'm extremely tired, and I'll be seventy when this kid, okay, well, he's not going to college, but you know. I hadn't even begun to recover from putting the dog down. *I really don't know if I can do this, honey. This is a lot.*

We could try to look for some people who want a baby, Dan said.

We both knew nobody wanted a baby right then. Yes, babies were still being born, not as often, and many of them didn't last a week, but you heard stories like this, about abandoned babies. Even if you might have once wanted a baby, our new world has gone a long way for promoting birth control. I mean, there's really only one kind of birth control now, but still. People try. It's just too hard to have babies.

Dan took the baby out of the bucket. He was filthy and scrawny but Dan was very tender with him, wiped a smudge of dirt off his nose with some spit. *How old do you think he is*?

Less than a year?

He had that thin, wispy baby hair, and he could sit up on his own, but he wasn't walking.

Okay, well, first things first, let's get this guy fed.

We had absolutely not one thing that anyone would ever feed a baby. We had, at that time, been doing fine for ourselves with the potatoes, carrots, berries, chicken eggs, and a few other things we had managed to grow, but we mostly drank water. Sometimes milk when we could get it. One of our neighbors had a goat, but he was stingy with his trades. Not that we had anything resembling a baby bottle either. We knew we could find some way to improvise on that, but the actual food part was going to be a little more challenging. Dan saw my look of worry and said, *Listen, let's just get something in him right now, and we'll worry about nutrition later.* So we filled a little plastic bag with water (there were still plenty of plastic bags, there will always be plenty of plastic bags) and poked a teeny hole in it and brought it up to his mouth and he figured that out like a champ, which was a huge relief.

Maybe we won't totally kill him, I said.

Nah. I think, at worst, we'll only partially kill him, Dan said.

Some months before that.

Early on in the transition, there were differences of opinion on whether or not the change was permanent. Dan and I were ourselves somewhat divided. I held out hope as long as I could; Dan insisted he knew almost before it even happened. When I asked why he didn't tell me, he said he did, and reminded me that we'd talked at length about the end of oil years before. But another one of our jokes is, You know I don't listen. My memory is that I just didn't think it would happen in our lifetime even if I was listening. Of course, much had been known about the damage we'd already done to the planet, but day to day, weird weather changes or even these extreme weather events that were obviously happening more often didn't indicate that we had as little time left as we did. The news, and the government, at that point, weren't predicting this exactly. Maybe they were trying not to be alarmist, who knows, but regardless of the warnings and preparations we were all encouraged to start setting in place; it seemed more precautionary than anything else, like an earthquake emergency kit, at worst, stuff to tide you over until FEMA came or whatever. Except FEMA wasn't coming. I'm not saying it wasn't alarming, but if you've lived a number of decades taking your cushy lifestyle for granted, there's just a level of denial that you might not ever shake until it happens. Anyway, as soon as we—let's say—agreed that the change was permanent, the first thing we did was claim the empty house I'd always admired over on Cambridge. It had been empty ever since we moved to the neighborhood and I eyed it every single day when I was out walking the dog wondering why no one ever moved in or put a for-sale sign on it. It would have been a two-million-dollar house easy back then. I asked Dan if he thought maybe it was haunted. *Everything's haunted*, he said. I'd always thought my grandparents' house was haunted, not like ghosts trying to scare us out or anything like in a movie, but just a general feeling that in an old home like that, there was, well, something. As Dan pointed out, plenty of people had always preferred old homes, the difference was that now no one was in much position to be choosy about it. He also reminded me about all the foreclosures and short sales, abandoned malls and ruined river towns back before any of this happened. I hadn't forgotten. It was hard not to feel a little bit badly about all the claiming of things you knew people may have lost due to one difficulty or another. But options were extremely limited. Even if we'd stayed in the apartment we were in, it's not like we'd have kept paying rent.

But back to that baby.

Dan and I always shared a sort of dark sense of humor, but with the world the way it was now, and death being more or less in your face on a daily basis, we were kidding but not kidding about whether or not we might kill the baby. We really didn't know if we could keep a child alive. We had three dogs, an outside cat (I'm allergic), and four chickens by then, and we hadn't killed them yet, but a human baby we were less sure about. So, you know, when in doubt, make jokes about worst-possible outcomes, we say.

We named him Samuel Wesley, for our dads.

As soon as he drank that water, his cheeks started to pink up. We had some hard-boiled eggs, so we mashed one up real good with some potatoes and hoped he was ready for solid food, and he was. He was very ready. We used rags for diapers and we put him down that night and he slept—you know what he slept like.

At the end of that first day, as soon as he fell asleep, we both cried. We also laughed, but we cried.

We would learn a few months later that he was probably closer to three than one, when he started talking a lot and told us his name was actually Manny.

Before.

We moved to Brooklyn from Austin ten years ago, where we'd spent three long years while Dan was getting his MFA in sculpture. (Yes, I was that one who didn't love Austin.) I had grown up in Manhattan, so I anticipated some financial challenges, but Dan had never lived in New York. We agreed to stay for a few years before settling down in some nice Midwestern college town. Rents were just about to force us out (even sooner than anticipated) when the apocalypse hit. Ha! Suddenly that seems funny. I'm fifty now and Dan is forty-eight and long before all this went down we had sort of permanently tabled the kid issue and we were fine with that.

A couple of blocks from us, there was a so-called playground on a series of lots that had been cleared for a new condo complex that never happened. It had once been the home of an artist who'd moved there in the '70s, over the decades repairing and festooning the house with all manner of scavenged treasures, creating stained-glass windows from broken bottles, mosaics made of glass, tile, and scrap metal; after nearly forty years, the artist was evicted and most of his work dismantled, leaving, more or less, just the façade with a giant hole in the center. The work of "restoring" the building into condos never came to pass. So what had been piles of debris in a hole in the ground became what some people liked to call a "progressive learning project." This wasn't a brand-new concept; I'd seen a documentary about a playground like this and I even remember thinking it was a cool idea at the time, that we'd landed in an era of overprotecting our kids and this was a sort of interesting backlash. Basically, it was the opposite of every safe, considered, modern playground ever, where the kids could build fires, roll around in mud puddles if they felt like it, construct things out of donated wood scraps and whatever kind of rusty junk turned up there on any given day. Think: if someone suddenly swapped out the sign at the dump with one that said THE PLAYGROUND on it. There was adult supervision, or to be more accurate, there were adults present. Supervision was questionable.

Dan and I walked past it one day and remembered the structure in its glory, having met the artist just before his eviction. *Where do you think he is now?* I asked. The last we heard he was going to live with his son.

Dan shrugged. *I dunno, he was already old.*

Imagine if he saw this, I said.

Think about it, though. *He raised kids in this crazy building. It had holes in the roof and no heat. He might have preferred this over condos. I do. I'd bring my kids here.*

Good thing we don't have kids.

Before, during, after.

I still write. People have been writing since—well, since caves. Now, having used up most of what was on hand, we're back to making paper when we can, though my efforts usually prove too crumbly to write on. Dan suggested parchment, but when I asked how parchment was made and he said from animal intestines, I said I would sooner stop writing than deal with that. The point is, paper is just one of a million luxuries that we have to work for if we want it. I write with one of my dad's old fountain pens and ink I make with whatever I can and I write on whatever relatively flat and thin item I can find on any given day. I had started a novel based on me and my mom (again), which seemed a little less pressing post-apocalypse. But I didn't want her to be forgotten, and I didn't think anyone was much interested in hearing contemporary stories about epic killer flus just yet. For a period of time I wrote flash fiction on the windows with a dry-erase marker and then one morning when that was dried up I used a Sharpie, which did not please my husband as much as it pleased my two readers. (I wrote them backward.) It was an original window.

Sometimes I think about how our hierarchy of needs,

you know, the Maslow thing, changes according to the times. Which is to say that the top of that triangle keeps stretching a bit to include things like ever-new technologies we suddenly can't function without, or you know, things like fame and prestige. And so, when ecological change comes, as it will ('sup, dinosaurs?), and has again, and some of us have to move down the needs pyramid, from the eighty-dollar-candle level down through the working-out-your-issues-with-your-mother level and into the eating-and-breathing-and-staying-warm levels. These other needs are maybe not gone from your mind so much as less of an immediate priority. Novels become less of a priority. Novels become, on occasion, kindling. Not in my house. But it happens.

When Manny was four or five.

Briefly, before, Dan and I had considered adopting a child. Ultimately we tabled the discussion, primarily due to the financial concern of having no finances, and things changed, as is clear that they do, and time made our tabling into a decision. Enter Manny, another decision we only sort of made, and yes, that his arrival came when finances were of no concern to anyone was not lost on us.

When Manny was about four or five, he began to have nightmares we were ill-prepared to help him with, or I was, anyway. He would wake up screaming and all we could ever tease out was *Mommy* and *Daddy*; we'd run in to his room and tell him, *Daddy's right here, Mommy's right here,* and he'd say, *No, no, no!* and shake his head to try to get it out and scream until his little voice was hoarse. He never once told us what the dreams were, only that they were always the same.

In a quiet moment one morning while Manny was eating breakfast, Dan asked him if he remembered anything from before he came to us. He nodded, but his expression was inscrutable, anything in the range between I don't want to talk about it to Duh. He kept eating, mashed potatoes that particular morning. *Do you want to tell us about it* didn't seem like the right question. *Do you miss your mommy and daddy?* Dan asked him.

Sometimes, he said.

This was one of the only times I saw Dan cry, or try not to. *I miss mine too,* Dan said, and Manny gave him a hug, which was about the sweetest thing you could ever see, except at a certain point Manny was ready to be done hugging, and he patted Dan on the back like you do when you're being hugged by someone from that other department at work who thinks you're better friends than you are.

A few years before.

When we first got to Brooklyn we rented a sunny and cute but modest apartment in Clinton Hill; they filmed some scenes from *Girls* on our corner a few weeks after we moved in. (*Girls*—a TV show—I hope I don't have to explain what TV is—anyway you surely know what a show is, and this was a show about angsty twentysomething women trying to figure their shit out in upscale coffee shops and bougie boho apartments—which I realize sounds like I didn't like it, but I actually loved it; in my forties I hadn't yet forgotten how much it sucked to be twenty-anything.) So we were deep in new-era Brooklyn. Around the world, Brooklyn had become a thing, a label to put on things, synonymous with everything-old-is-new-again style coolness, but it was still sweet and it was still Brooklyn and frankly, yes, I happily paid three bucks for a blood orange donut that tasted like paradise. That shit was good, a small luxury I could actually afford. I was happier than I'd been in years. Dan has excellent fixing-up skills and even our little Brooklyn apartment was evidence of that. He built me a window seat. I asked for a simple little bench and he gave me a window seat that looked like it had been there from the beginning, with trim and everything. I make curtains and quilts and pillows, and I was never a fantastic seamstress but I get the job done and these days it is not hard to impress anyone who comes over. (Post-apoc, after a lot of sewing by hand, I finally located an antique sewing machine with a foot pedal, which is the kind of item people scooped up pretty quickly.) Honestly, like most of us, I'm happy just to have blankets. Because you know why blankets? No heat.

During.

Government, when it still existed, was, well, insert your own joke here. It wasn't what you'd call functional. The pre-apocalyptic mayor was still alive, and he had tried to set up some guidelines before all electronic communication ended, but there was no way to stop things like looting, for just one example. For the most part, this wasn't just because people could—there was a genuine need. Looting eventually just became known as "shopping." It wasn't entirely uncivilized, but we were definitely making new rules, and on a certain level it was still pretty much every person for every person's self, and it brought out the best and the worst in people. Places like Target were rough when they still had anything. I saw a woman with a bloody escalator print on her face one day so . . . yeah. I wasn't about to fight over the last, partial ream of printer paper. Still, we held on to our iPhones. The last of our photos were in there, plus a couple voicemails, and we knew that was the end of those, but we just couldn't. We couldn't.

We followed the news, while it still existed as it once had (arguably, the news business had stopped existing as it once had a couple decades prior). As per usual, the heads made a lot of predictions that have not come to pass (ranging from widespread violence to zombies, no lie), but the two things they got most right was that as soon as the power was all used up, many, many people would die, and that we could expect a steep increase in crime almost immediately. Most people had the good sense to get in touch with their friends and family around the country and say some sort of preliminary good-byes, not knowing how or when or if ever we'd be in touch again. That sucked a lot.

One afternoon during.

Walking Manny home from school one afternoon, I asked about his day. He said it was okay. *Just okay?* I asked.

I got a time-out.

You did, I said. *How come?*

Manny sighed. *I yelled at Miko.*

Oh, I said. I didn't ever want to say anything until I felt clear on what happened, and generally, Manny just didn't want to say much of anything. We learned quickly that information gathering was a delicate process of acting like we weren't trying to do what we were doing. Questions were often met with silence and blank stares.

Why did you yell at her? Were you playing a game? Did she say something mean?

Nah, he finally said. *Miko and I are good.*

I wondered if anything happened at all, if this was just one of those kid phases. We got home and he went quietly to his room. It was then that I realized that in the two years he'd been with us, he had never once called us Mom or Dad or even Janie or Dan. He had never called us anything.

After the apocalypse but before the baby.

So we wheeled all our shit over to the Cambridge house in a grocery cart. A hundred and thirty-seven trips. We had been living in a fifth-floor walkup, which had been fine when we still had power and heat, not so much anymore. Everyone was exhausted as it was. The house had been empty for years, and it had a little patch of dirt in the back where we could plant. It was what people were doing. (Occasionally you heard about someone coming back after some years to reclaim a claimed house, and those stories often had grim endings too, but the only reclaim we knew of around here actually ended with the original owners reoccupying an unused part of the house. It wasn't uncommon to share space, which was one way of easing the burden of maintaining a house.)

We put up curtains and laid down rugs and made it our home. No one ever came around to say otherwise. (Well, except for the new-era carpetbaggers, but that was a ways off.) There was very little acreage, really, less than some of the brownstones, to tell you the truth, but it had a sweet front porch. In Brooklyn. It was a house from before brownstones. From like farm times. Anyway, we got creative with the way we used the land we did have (e.g. no need for that driveway anymore!), and also there were still plenty of community gardens and empty lots on which to start more community gardens.

That first spring, we started with just potatoes and carrots. That got old fast, even considering we still had salt. Thank god for salt. Now and again someone would come around selling random things that included spices, which always pleased Dan, but I never liked spicy foods anyway. I did, however, like variety, which was not currently happening.

It was, surprisingly, a few years before things got really rough for us. If you had been taking medication for anything, well, yeah, that ran out fast. God, I wish I'd thought of going off my SSRIs a little sooner. That was an adjustment for both of us. There was a time when we joked that meds were the foundation of our marriage. But we dealt with it. There were moods. There was what Dan still calls the Crying Year. We were never hoarders, but we did have a lot of stuff, and you'd be surprised how things you don't even think of as being resources are resources. Yes, some things were more obvious than others, needles and thread and fabric and buttons. I maybe had two or three boxes full of all the above, but it has gone a long way for us in our textile needs. Thrift stores became co-ops and repositories of sorts, people volunteering in shifts to keep things under control; there wasn't a shortage of clothes, thanks to the decades of severely underpaid garment workers producing at the rate they once did, but it was still a finite resource. Hand tools and every last little nail or screw. We also made a detailed inventory of what we had that could be used or reused in ways we had previously not thought of. Records, CDs, magazines, old appliances, lots and lots of odd things got repurposed.

Many, many millions of people died almost immediately. If you were in a hospital when the power ended and you had anything worse than a broken bone, you were pretty much screwed. It was hard to take the dogs for a walk in the park without one of them sniffing up on what would turn out to be some part of a person. The phrase *a walk in the park* came to mean something very different. It was often traumatic. One time on a longer walk we saw a faded handmade sign under the Williamsburg Bridge, with a big pink breast cancer ribbon that read TEAM CAROL. This kind of hope for a cure of anything was long gone. But really, it happened everywhere. What used to be the evening news, stuff that happened in remote parts of the world, or parts of town you tried to avoid, something secured inside a screen, was now daily life for everyone everywhere. Probably in some of those parts, where people had been living in huts the whole time, they were laughing at us, or they would if they even knew what was going on.

It was very, very hard. If there's one certain thing in this new era, it's that the only thing you can be sure of is that day to day, stuff will come up that hasn't come up before. You think you've got all the basics worked out, how to make fire, where to get food and other needed supplies, and then another superstorm of some kind hits (actually we went back to just calling them storms again, very few of them weren't super) and you're set back again and you have to think of new ways to rebuild or get what you need.

But for relatively healthy people, marginally creative or industrious people, doable, and Dan and I were always a good team and we liked the quiet time together (even if there wasn't ever a ton of spare time). Neighbors were neighborly. We got to know them. We helped each other where we could. Not seeing our friends in other cities or even, you know, other boroughs, sucked. It still sucks. There are a lot of people we don't see and don't even hear of. There are new mail delivery services, but these are extremely slow, and sometimes the deliverers or the horses die before they get there. I was always grateful to hear that someone was fine, but I felt a pang of melancholy whenever these missives came, and sometimes I wondered if it was better to just try not to think about it at all. Was denial, in these times, really such a bad thing? Complete, blazing consciousness twenty-four hours a day seemed like it would just take you right out. I had been enjoying spending more time with my childhood best friend until traveling to and from Manhattan to see each other suddenly became a day trip. So we write when we can. But when letters come with news of the loss of a parent that happened weeks earlier, the powerlessness to be a real friend is painful.

Maybe a year or so after continuing not to accidentally kill Manny.

It was around the time that Manny started to come into himself, learning to walk, and becoming a whole small person, that Dan and I started to have some pretty big disagreements when it came to parenting. Dan's general idea was that we didn't really need to worry since the worst was already here, which was not an argument that persuaded me. It's not like I'm pro-worrying. Dan might disagree with that, but I don't think I randomly worry about stuff. It's just that even walking down the street is risky now in ways that it hadn't been in the fifty years I've been alive, not even back in the '70s. Wildlife is a new thing around here. I remember once, years ago, before, there was a raccoon outside our window on our (fifth-floor) fire escape on Classon and it scared the bejesus out of me (a) that it was just out there staring at me and (b) uh, raccoons in Brooklyn. No idea. So maybe it shouldn't have been so surprising when we started to see more critters like raccoons, possums (the worst), foxes, deer, of course, and coyotes. One time I could have sworn I saw a javelina over by what was left of the Atlantic Center. (Dan said it was probably just a wild hog. Still. Wild hog. Where Target used to be.) The point is, the wildlife is just one thing. The streets are in disrepair. There's crime. There's disease. And you're pretty much on your own when it comes to dealing with this stuff, even though communities have come together on a micro level to try to manage it all as best we can. Dan's point is that if we know shit's going to happen, why should we waste our time worrying about it? And that makes sense to me on a theoretical level, but in practice, it is much harder to do something as simple as let your kid go play outside without worrying.

People always worried about their kids playing outside, though, Dan said.

Sure, I said, *but back then, there wasn't anything to worry about.*

So you're saying, if we'd had a kid back then, you wouldn't have worried.

Fine, I totally would have. But not like this.

We had many conversations like this, and Manny lived his life like there wasn't anything weird about it, because what did he know about how things used to be, and he had some little friends, because it was Brooklyn, you know, there were kids. Manny's school was the current equivalent of a one-room schoolhouse, sort of a co-op school, if you will, where each of the parents would come in and teach one subject that they knew about. I taught English, Dan taught art, and we tried to include practical skills, sort of a modern home ec, though we still hadn't come to a collective mind on that, it was kind of catch-as-catch-can. We used a couple of rooms in the abandoned elementary school over on Gates. It was loose, you know, we were working without a lot of the old resources, and we had to go on a certain amount of faith that we weren't misguiding them too much.

The playground now.

So, yeah. We got a kid. And Dan made the case for letting him go to the playground, to which I very reluctantly agreed. As I said, there was adult supervision, kind of like at our co-op school, parents took turns, but it was minimal, and it was understood that any and all harm that came to your child was your own responsibility. It was, absolutely, obviously dangerous, but it was considered educational, and I didn't disagree that there were potential benefits. But Jesus Christ. I was really not a fan of the idea of my kid playing with broken bottles like they were Legos. Our compromise was that Dan would only let Manny play there on the days when he was supervising, which, well, if you know Dan, it's not so much that I didn't believe he'd keep his eyes open, but more that he'd just watch and cheer while Manny ran the hurdles over barbed wire. There was never a time when Manny didn't come home with some sort of scrape on him, usually no big deal, but when he came back with a huge cut on his forehead because he'd been playing Frisbee with a rusty hubcap, I was pretty miffed with my husband.

Like we don't have enough problems, you couldn't have helped him find something a little smaller to toss around?

We chose between that and playing catch with half a brick. I made a call.

I'm not sure this comes under the heading of learning.

Well, but what if it's just play?

Fine, but there are already enough hazards as it is, you have to go make more?

Janie—he's fine.

He was fine. I didn't want to argue.

But things reached a peak when Manny came home from school one day with a broken ankle. He'd been so excited to tell us about how well his show-and-tell had gone (he showed-and-told about how he helped make a type of building block out of CDs by cutting into their edges) that he ran ahead of Dan and fell into a Volkswagen-sized pothole. Dan and I barely spoke a word to one another until after we got him bandaged up and splinted and put to bed. But this time I just couldn't keep it in.

This is totally your fault, I said to Dan.

Up until this time, we had never called each other a name, never yelled (there were raised voices a time or two), never openly blamed the other for anything, even if maybe we thought it once in a while. We were very proud of our fair and reasonable conflict-resolution skills.

Dan didn't know what to say. It's not that he doesn't have a temper in him, I know he does. It's just that up until then, his temper, when it did come up, had always been directed elsewhere. The usual stuff: politics, shitty drivers, assholes on the subway, family members who suck.

Yeah, I said that, I said. *I'm mad.*

How is it my fault that there are potholes in the street?

The potholes aren't your fault. You told him he could run when he felt like running.

That's not what I told him.

Yes, you did.

No, I told him to look where he was going when he ran.

Which is the same as telling him it's okay to run.

Okay, yes, there is an assumption of running. He's a kid. He's going to run.

Well, I think we should have been more specific about where and how to run.

You're being ridiculous.

No, I'm not! You can't be so lackadaisical!

No kid is going to stop before he runs, he's just going to run. Kids run. They fall down, they get up.

But he didn't get up! What if it was worse? What if he fell on his head?

But he didn't.

But what if he did?

I don't want to do this what if thing anymore, Janie. We're so far past what if we're in all if all the time.

He got me there. I would have argued anyway, but I paused too long.

I'm going to bed, Dan said.

For a while after that.

I tended to go from zero to worst-case scenario in about three thought leaps, and worst-case scenario was always that Dan would leave. This was true whether we were in conflict about socks on the floor or bigger things like money issues. *I'm not leaving you*, he would say when I cried early on in a fight. It sometimes helped but once during this prolonged rough patch he added, *Where would I go?* which I knew was meant humorously but I tend to lose my sense of humor at these times and I couldn't shake the idea that he'd been considering where he might go. For weeks, we continued to have conversations that resolved nothing until we more or less stopped speaking. We had never stopped speaking for so much as an hour in the past. And then just as Manny's cast was about to come off, he got into this thing where he started plucking feathers off the chickens. While they were alive. We didn't notice for a while, he wasn't plucking them bald, but when we found a box of chicken feathers under his bed we were pretty sure he hadn't just picked them up off the ground. We actually saved those for pillows and things. So now we had another problem, which was that our problem was causing him problems. That much seemed obvious. We tried talking to him about it.

Sweetie, you understand that hurts the chicken, right? Try to think of it as if we pulled your hair out, but kind of worse.

We could see that he understood.

So, you won't do this any more? Manny nodded. His expression indicated remorse, though there was something else to it we couldn't name. He stopped plucking chicken feathers but soon enough he started spitting at his teachers at school. Generally, we tried to practice patience and tolerance for behavior problems at the co-op, there was hardly a kid there that didn't have one kind of issue or another and didn't act out sometimes, but when he spit on another kid, that kid's mom had a little less patience and tolerance than some, and she wanted to suspend Manny. People got sick and died from spit these days. (Later, the other boy's mom turned around completely, apologizing to us when her kid got in trouble for biting.) And we tried explaining to Manny that if they didn't happen to die, it hurt people's feelings too.

I know, he said.

Why do you think you've been doing these things, sweetie? I asked.

Don't ask him that. Jesus, Dan said. *He doesn't know.*

Well, I think maybe he does. Do you? Can you remember why you spit on Kerouac today?

Silence.

Did he do something to you?

Manny shook his head no.

Were you mad at him?

He shrugged. *Just mad.*

We explained that spitting wasn't okay, that it could transmit germs and disease, and that also it just wasn't nice.

He knows it's not nice, Janie. That's why he's doing it.

Okay, fine, but then why does he want to not be nice? Why do you not want to be nice to your friends, Manny?

I am nice to my friends. Everyone's not my friend.

Sure, they are, sweetie.

No, they're not, Janie. Don't tell him that. Is everyone your friend?

It's different for kids.

What universe did you grow up in?

I grew up here.

Were you friends with everyone?

Of course not. But there's a different school of thought now. There's conflict resolution.

Listen, you can't make him like who he doesn't like. We should be teaching him to trust his instincts. If he doesn't feel good about a person . . .

He should try to get to know them instead of spitting on them.

That's not how childhood works.

Stop it, Manny said. *Stop yelling.*

We hadn't even realized we were yelling. So, we stopped. Talking didn't immediately take its place.

Somewhere in here.

The thing that seemed to help Manny most was that he had made a motley band of little and not-so-little friends at the playground, with whom he seemed to share a kinship that I feel hard-pressed to describe in a way that would do it service. They ranged in age from maybe four or five on the young end all the way up to about fourteen; together they seemed grubbily genderless and raceless, more like their existence as an entity defined them more than their parts. Whatever scrape he came home with was usually counterbalanced by an energy and pride I never saw from any of the encouragement Dan or I ever gave him. One day he came home with a toy boat he'd made with a level of detail that I can only describe as Viking ship meets kayak meets some guy on a porch in the hills with a whittling knife and a straw in his teeth. Even Dan was mystified as to its construction, examining it from all sides and marveling at the apparent lack of any sort of nails or glue. It was the kind of thing I'd have Instagrammed the shit out of once upon a time.

Several weeks after the plucking and the spitting.

We need couples therapy, I said, pulling up the bedcovers. The silence had gotten to me. I'm a talker.

There's no couples therapy anymore.

Well, I know, but we need something. We need help. Do you want to fix this?

I guess.

I guess is never the right answer when you're asking your husband if he's interested in saving your marriage. But I know Dan well enough to know that *I guess* here means yes, I want to save the marriage but I am really not looking forward to the effort involved.

Kerouac's mom used to be a shrink, I said.

Erg.

I know.

Wasn't she like, into some weird thing?

Oh yeah. I think so.

This was one of those moments where we both knew what the other was talking about even though we couldn't remember the specifics other than that we had thought it was hilarious at the time. We might have laughed if we hadn't just started speaking again.

Do we know anyone else?

I heard there was some kind of something in Queens.

Queens!

It's not that far.

Can't we just try to work this out ourselves? I mean, you know this is about your mom, at the bottom of it, right?

Does it always have to be about my mom? Couldn't it be about your mom, one time?

Mmm. No.

You never even knew my mom.

Have we ever worked through anything where it didn't turn out to be about your mom?

It was about your dad or stepdad a time or two.

Yeah, okay. But that's not what's happening here.

Dammit.

I know.

I really hoped I'd abandoned my abandonment issues post-apocalypse.

We're still us.

I sighed.

I'm not leaving you.

Queens. He might as well have said Alaska. It wasn't that far to go to save my marriage, and for crying out loud, there were still Jehovah's Witnesses who came to the door. And

I knew they didn't live around here. Yes, I knew people still practiced religion, that wasn't so surprising, but you'd think there'd be a few less people willing to go out and witness. I've asked them where they came from. We always invited them in for whatever we might have to offer. None of those Witnesses have ever come from anywhere closer than Coney Island and some even from Jersey and beyond. The point is, those people had to do all the same things we did just to eat, and yet they still had this other thing that mattered to them enough to walk all those miles.

I'm willing, Dan said.

Fine, I said.

In the therapy era.

So we walked to Kew Gardens. Almost three hours each way. Could have been worse. But Dan also had to walk there and back once just to make the appointment. I wish I could say it was worth it. But post-apocalyptic therapy turned out to be . . . I think they're working out some kinks. I was always on board with behavior therapy, but this was a version of it that I had some issues with. The therapist gave us several exercises and told us to come back the following week with a report. One of the exercises involved taking off our clothes (to reveal ourselves) standing in the middle of the street (to stand our ground) and taking turns screaming our greatest need (to show our vulnerability) to the other.

So yeah, we didn't do any of that.

We did go talk to Kerouac's mom, which turned out to be considerably more helpful than we expected. We asked her what her practice was, because we'd heard rumors (sand therapy, whatever that was, encounter groups, psychodrama), but she said, *We just talk. I was into puppets once.* She motioned to a puppet on a high shelf that looked to me like the ventriloquist dummy from that old Anthony Hopkins movie *Magic*, which likely you haven't seen, so consider yourself lucky. It was hard to imagine that being helpful in any way other than facilitating nightmares. It was pretty loose. She asked us about what our lives were like before. We told her that pre-apocalypse, pre-Manny, we'd always been very compatible, that we had certainly had our own issues that we'd done some work on in individual therapy over the years. I mentioned that I'd written and published quite a few short stories about my issues with my mom, but that it seemed kind of meaningless now, that fiction itself sometimes seemed meaningless.

I still read, she said.

That whole thing about the hierarchy of needs, you know, when the apocalypse comes, yes, it was true that we stayed pretty close to the bottom. Only now does it occur to me to think about how back before we used gas and electricity in the first place that of course people had issues—whatever they might have called them—and of course they dealt with them in some way. Even not dealing with problems is a way of dealing with them. Women once had to beat their clothes on rocks to get them clean, or spend an entire day baking one loaf of bread, all while wearing nineteen petticoats or something, point being, there might have been a woman or two or three who were like, *Maybe I'd prefer to go hunting, or at least to be asked*, but who didn't ever say that out loud, because women didn't say a lot of things out loud then, and/or they probably knew what the reaction would be if they did dare and so then they became sullen and resentful, which maybe affected their kids, and their marriages, even though nothing was ever done about any of it. And so now, it's a new time, it's not like either of those times exactly, but it's a new time that's still populated by humans, many of whom (and perhaps an even greater number in Brooklyn) have a long pre-apocalyptic history of *processing their feelings*. I italicized that because how could you not. I was one of them, and apparently I'm still one of them.

Then this happened.

Talking with Kerouac's mom, we had negotiated that once a week or so I would go along to the playground with Dan and Manny. I generally stayed away because watching the kids navigate that treacherous place tied my stomach in knots, and sometimes, when it was possible, we picked and chose when it came to daily brutalities. Dan hadn't seen it quite that way, so he had been happy to do it, but in the interest of our relationship and family togetherness, I went. It was the day after an ice storm. Every single thing in the playground was covered in ice that day, saw blades, rusted bicycle chains, pipes, auto parts, and with the sun coming down and the kids taking turns "snowboarding" off a ramp they'd fashioned from the roof of a car, there was a rough but undeniable beauty to the scene. We left with Manny unscathed and exhilarated to recap for us how he'd gone down the ramp six times and landed on his feet every time. Seeing his joy and his confidence in action, I definitely got it in a way I hadn't before, though it didn't compel me to spend extra time there. We did also see a boy nearly crack his skull falling off that same ramp. But it was a bit of a triumph for all of us, and it felt like our spirits were on their way up.

And then on the way home, on the curb not far from our house, sticking out from under some kind of tarp, we found two girls, huddled together like something out of Pompeii, except with ice. By this time we had already seen any number of grim things, unimaginably grim. Some part of me knew immediately that these girls were gone, but you don't ever want to know that. They might have been ten years old, maybe eleven. Manny moved toward them and I tried to pull him away but he kneeled down next to them to look more closely.

I know them, he said. *They used to watch us outside the playground sometimes. Didn't want to come in*. Manny stood up but held his gaze on their faces.

I wish I could describe what I saw in him in that moment. It was something you might easily mistake for stoic, but to me it was like he was holding every feeling that existed at once. I bent down and when I put my hand on a back to see if they were breathing, I felt the blanket crackle under my mitten and the air went out of me. Their faces were purple. Their eyes were closed. I prayed to something that they'd been asleep when they died. I couldn't imagine what freezing to death felt like but considering how scrawny they were, they were probably on the edge of starving to death as it was. It occurred to me that it could have even been both at the same time. Either way, they were sixteen shades of purple.

They were sisters, Manny said.

I had mostly been holding it together until this point, and these were not the first deaths we'd seen, but I lost it big time, and I threw myself on them, these frozen dead girls I didn't know, like maybe I could somehow heat them back up to life. Manny put his hand on my shoulder, and Dan bent down to put his arms around me before gently pulling me away.

How are we supposed to make sense of this? I said.

There's no sense to be made, Dan said.

Moments like these, which were now more or less daily (not quite this horrific every day, but there was usually some greater or lesser loss we were forced to acknowledge/step over/deal with on most days), tended to make me wonder if there was a force that was actively evil. I mean, I don't really believe that. Everyone understood that this was how things were now. (Everyone except some super religious people who were as sure as ever that sin was behind all this and, despite everything, seemed weirdly pleased to see a version of their predictions come to pass. Thankfully we didn't have that much contact with these types.) But this didn't make it any less painful.

It was hard to know what to do next. People had taken to burying the dead in parks, but we knew the ground would be too hard for a while yet.

Let's take them to the fires, Manny said.

You know about the fires? I said to Manny, tossing a horrified look to Dan. I hope the idea is self-explanatory. It isn't pleasant, and even if it makes a certain amount of sense—in the old days I'd definitely have wanted to be cremated—in the new days it sometimes felt like something out of a concentration camp. Dan pointed out that the main difference between now and then was that we didn't have to see it then.

Like a lot of things, he said.

So we wrapped them in a blanket and strapped them onto our dolly—yeah—and walked the few blocks over to one of the closest lots where the fires were done. (There were, um, a lot of these lots. Think corner deli numbers. For a while they held them every Wednesday and Sunday morning, like it was a farmer's market—in fact, some of them were on those exact same lots—but thankfully the numbers slowed down so it went back to just . . . as needed. And you never didn't know because the smell didn't go away unless they'd been out for a while. You got used to that. Kind of.) We arrived there to find the fire not quite out, which we were grateful for even though we knew what it meant. There were times of flu and other things when the fires seemed to never go out at all.

Let's say a prayer, Dan said, and I grumbled and told him to say it, and he said *I think you should say it*. I knew what he was trying to do. Neither of us believed in god and I didn't see the point but he gave me one of those looks that he gives me and so I said, *Please look over these girls*, and resisted the urge to add, *O great nothing*. I paused, hoping something nicer would come to me, but I couldn't think of anything before I started sobbing again, too hard to speak even if I did have some idea what to say. I unwrapped the blanket and kissed them on their purple foreheads. Dan picked them up to lay them on the fire.

You don't have to look, he said.

I do, I said.

There was a physical feeling of weight, in these moments, that overused metaphor we talked about time and again in the writing workshops that I used to teach, but you really did feel like you may just as well have strapped all these bodies on your backs while at the same time continuing to go about the business of not being one of them. And yet I felt, as Manny clearly did as well, that turning away wasn't the right thing either, that they deserved witness. Manny held his arm out toward the girls as they began to burn and made a peace sign.

Manny's seventh birthday.

About a month before the day we called his birthday, Dan and I started planning. It took a little time to gather what you needed for any kind of a special occasion. No one was terribly sorry that the era of over-the-top kids' birthday parties was over, even a couple of the parents who'd given one or two. One couple we knew had once tried to rent out the entire Brooklyn Bridge. *They laughed at us when we called*; *That's not a thing, they told us*, they said, laughing. *We thought money could make anything a thing. And now money isn't even a thing.* Birthday parties were sometimes hard enough as it was; that was also the era of "everyone is included" and "you have to have separate cakes for kids with special dietary needs and you're considered rude and thoughtless if you don't." The thing is that kids aren't stupid, and they always know when they aren't really wanted, so even if they were lucky enough that no one was openly mean, they could still, you know, look around a room and see what was going on. Anyway, I asked Manny what he wanted for his birthday (requests were always taken, what was ultimately produced obviously depended on many factors) and he asked for a Bowie knife and requested that his playground friends come over for whatever, he didn't really care. And when I asked him if he knew what a Bowie knife was and what he thought he was going to do with it, the look that came over his not-yet-seven-year-old face—and it was not dramatic in any way—was one that might best be described as ancient. I felt very much in that moment that he believed that I just didn't get it.

He's like a cat, I told Dan later.

What are you talking about?

I wasn't sure how to explain it now that I'd said it out loud. Maybe easiest to say that I loved Manny deeply, but that I was a dog person.

Where do you think we could find a Bowie knife, Dan asked.

I think we are not going to try to find a Bowie knife.

Oh, come on. He plays with bricks and bottles.

Aware. Not up for discussion. No knife.

I tried to make a cake of sorts. I'd gotten okay at making a type of galette out of any kind of fruit, but I was set on making something like a real cake. Sadly without flour or sugar (we had baking powder, there will always be baking powder, think about the old days and how long you had that tin of baking powder; ours was practically vintage), my buttercream frosting did not make up the difference. It was truly inedible. I mean, technically it was edible, it wouldn't have made you sick. But no one could be blamed for not wanting to eat it. One of the playground moms was relieved no one was eating it because she wasn't going to let her kid eat that or anything else we served because she couldn't be sure that it hadn't at some point come into contact with a peanut. I was about to remind her where she sent her son to play every day when Manny shoved a piece of the cake into the face of a girl named Xiomara. She was about eight, and a foot taller than him; he was healthy but still undersized. Both of them laughed wildly, and a cake fight seemed like harmless fun until the first punch got thrown (we missed that), but in the middle of this possible rogue peanut conversation I sensed the commotion and turned to look at the tangle of kids now more or less in one big pile on the floor, kicking and punching and all of them laughing. On quick observation, it seemed the dads were standing by, amused, a couple of the mothers were yelling, and I was about to yell into that mix as well until Dan gently held me back. *It's fine*, he said.

It's not fine! It's so not fine! This is done! I yelled into the pile, pulling Manny out of the center by the arm. Some of the kids finally heard some of the yelling, and the pile broke apart quickly right after that, as did the party, but not one of those kids had any bit of visible remorse. Girls and boys alike, they parted with what I can only describe as baby bro hugs. Little recognitions.

The kids had said their good-byes before the gifts had been opened. Most of them were wrapped in one thing or another; scraps of fabric or plastic grocery bags (these things were generally given back after the gift was opened). None of them had any kind of gift tag on them, though Manny was easily able to guess who gave him what. One was an entire unused cylinder of writeable CDs. *My girl Xio knows what I like*, Manny said. We were scared to ask what *my girl* meant here. And of course, the best present of all, wrapped in a greasy piece of butcher paper tied with a fuzzy bit of twine, was a Bowie knife.

I tightened my jaw to avoid taking this out on Manny or starting another argument in front of him. We'd made a little progress in our therapy, we thought.

How about Dad and I just hold on to this for safekeeping for now, and we'll work out some arrangement later, I said. Dan nodded in concession. Manny scrunched up his face, but didn't argue.

A few weeks after that, while I was sleeping.

Dan had recently scored some coffee (declining to tell me exactly how) and got up before I did to make a pot. Coffee had become the stuff of much gossip: *I heard so-and-so got coffee, I heard what so-and-so did for that coffee.* Had there been any sort of news outlet at this point, you imagined that it would have been a top news story, SO-AND-SO OBTAINS COFFEE, INVESTIGATION FOLLOWS. The heavenly smell of the brew wafted into my dream and woke me up in my favorite way. I shuffled into the kitchen still in a hazy reverie about that little luxury we once took for granted, so when I reached for a mug and saw the writing on the kitchen window, for a hair of a second I thought those words were my own I'd just forgotten about. It took only another hair of a second to clue in, by which hair-second Dan was right there with me. *Oh,* was all I could think to say. *Set sail,* it said, with a big heart next to it. I'm pretty sure he kept it short because it was written in blood.

It's different now, Dan said. *Everyone can't stay.*

I had a million thoughts in my head about what we'd done wrong, what I'd done wrong, but some portion of my body knew this was right, and Dan did as well.

I knew that boat was a maquette, he said. *I knew it.*

I did too.

I looked at the note on the window again as though I might see something I missed, a PS.

It doesn't say he won't be back.

I knew he added that last thing because he thought maybe it was what I wanted to hear.

After Manny.

Dan had cleaned the window about a week after Manny left. He knew I never would have. I was staring at it when Dan came in. I could see the words there anyway.

I miss him.

I know.

I can't stop thinking about those girls.

You should try.

Where the fuck is god when this shit happens? Fuck that guy.

I had once had vague hopes that there might be a benevolent force in the world. That was before, obviously.

We could have let them live with us, I said. *If we'd just gotten home a little sooner that day, I mean.*

Don't think like that.

How do we not have PTSD? Do we have PTSD?

Maybe we wouldn't even know if we did at this point.

Did Manny have PTSD?

I don't think he did. I don't know. You know, there's no post-trauma now, it's all trauma all the time, maybe it just becomes something different. He seemed weirdly fine. I envy him.

Is this our fault?

What, no, of course not, how could it possibly be our fault?

I mean like, everyone's fault. All of it. Everyone who drove cars and used refrigerators and ate steak and whatever.

Oh. Well, yeah. But you're getting into . . .

Do *we have PTSD?*

I don't think we do. Or maybe everyone does now, sort of. Who knows. Or maybe it's true, what doesn't kill you makes you stronger?

Right then it seemed more like, What doesn't give you a psychotic break makes some other things a tiny bit easier to swallow.

Why aren't we just killing ourselves?

Honey, don't say that.

Seriously, people are.

I know.

And it's only going to get worse.

Not necessarily. I don't think we're going to know. We should probably not kill ourselves today.

Am I ever not going to be sad again?

I don't know. I hope so. I think so. I mean, I'm not that sad. Remember how sad I was when you met me?

That was over a dozen years ago, but it's hard to forget. I knew him for about a year before I ever saw him smile. By contrast he was Mary Poppins now.

We'll probably be too busy to be sad.

He was kind of right about that.

Some time later.

A few months after Manny left, I was cleaning out the chicken coop one morning when Dan came in and pulled me up to my feet.

Come on, he said, *let's take a walk. Down to the promenade.*

It's like an hour there and back, Dan. I have to finish this.

The chickens will hang in. Plus it's not even forty-five minutes. It's a beautiful day.

I groaned. It was a beautiful forty-degree day.

Fine.

When we opened the door, our white paint bucket was on the porch, the one Manny had arrived in, with a couple sunflowers in. *Look*, Dan said. *A sign!*

I loaned it to Eli next door, Dan. He brought it back. Also, we don't believe in signs.

Well, today I do. He grinned.

What's it a sign of, then?

I don't know everything. A sign that it's a good day for a walk.

I grumbled. We walked on the sunny side of the street. I stopped complaining after about a half mile. The sun felt good on my face and I remembered that now and again you could go for a walk and almost feel like things were just as they were before. People had really joined forces and did their part to maintain what they could; parks, residential structures, or at least non-high-rises. Some of the tallest buildings were looking worse for wear, but without elevators, they were pretty useless beyond the first couple floors. Many of the older ones were in better shape than you'd imagine, though we kind of didn't want to ever see the Empire State or the Chrysler Buildings again, just in case. The Promenade was as ever, dotted with people taking in the view, a charming turn-of-the-century tableau. The Brooklyn Bridge as well remained standing as it had since it was built. Without the vehicle traffic, it wasn't getting the wear and tear of previous years, and seeing it again after some time made me think about our history, what it must have been like then, building what was the tallest structure at the time. I could imagine that it was unthinkable to many that engineering could create such a thing, as unthinkable as it was to me now that we'd ever open our worlds up again in this same way. I wondered, surveying the bridge, the lower Hudson, the city skyline, how to process what I was even looking at—it seemed now like the industrial age was just a blip, in the long view, a folly. Like maybe we would have been better off not even knowing what was possible.

Do you think we even know what we're looking at? I asked Dan. He was always so patient when I got existential.

I think we're looking at history.

You mean like, the Freedom Tower is the Coliseum in that scenario? A ruin in the making?

Yeah. Maybe.

Okay, but does that tell you anything about our future?

That we'll probably have one?

Walking up Pierrepont Street on the way home, we ran into a teenager with a little table set up and a chalkboard that said COFFEE. We asked what she wanted in trade. *No trade*, she said. *If you like it, come back and we'll work something out next time.*

I already like it, Dan said to her. *Free coffee*, he said to me.

Not complaining, I said. Pretty sure I sounded like I was complaining though.

Hey, we have coffee and sunflowers today. What more do you want?

Electricity?

Can't have everything.

I know but I'm just a little tired.

That's what the coffee's for!

The next morning.

Dan made scrambled eggs with tomato for breakfast. We had food fresh from the garden every day. In comparison to what we'd been eating our whole lives, the flavor was so robust it made me think that whatever we'd been eating before wasn't even real food. I looked at the sunflowers, in a vase on the mantle. It was nice. But we had these moments, and then we worked.

Do you think things will ever get better? I asked him.

I think things will get different.

Different better?

Maybe this is *better. Maybe we don't know what's best*, Dan said.

He had me there.

But not knowing is the worst!

Dan shrugged. *Is what it is.*

I wish I could be more like you, I said.

Don't worry, I'll be stressed about something again soon enough and you'll be the one telling me everything's fine. You know how we always take turns. That hasn't changed.

That's true.

I wonder where Manny is right now.

I think he's fine. I think he went to the future.

Hard to imagine what Manny's future might end up looking like, could be anything from spaceships to hardcore back to nature, caves carved into mountains or something. Whatever it was, it felt beyond my vision, which was wide enough only to see Manny at the front of it, leading the way.

I wish I thought we were going to be here to see that, I said.

Me too, Dan said. *But think about this: If he's in it, that's gonna be one cool future.* He suggested we bring some eggs to the coffee girl, see if she was there again. I thought about it. The thought of another cup of coffee so soon was tempting enough to walk all that way.

I kind of feel like reading a book today, I said.

Interesting, Dan said. He knew I rarely read anymore. No time. Also everything was about before and it seemed like reading about before would just be like wishing for something I could never have. Plus, I always preferred to read about now anyway. But that wasn't currently an option.

Oh, whatever, I said. *Don't make anything of it.*

Coffee and books go well together, he said.

Maybe tomorrow, I said.

Notes for a Dad Story

Some things:

He had bad handwriting (as did his kid), but bad in a very distinctive way. Joked that it was because he was a doctor. (He was a PhD.) Always wrote with a felt-tip pen, not fine, always that and a mechanical pencil in his shirt pocket. Wrote and filed things on index cards, used scrap paper for notes; cut them into 3x5-ish pieces with the paper cutter he'd had since he was a kid. In his desk drawers, time-travel: fountain pens, ink bottles, a tape dispenser seemingly made of lead (*was* it made of lead?), a paperweight with the logo of the family business, photo corners from the 1930s, blotters from around the same time, an early calculator (she remembers the dad's excitement about this advancement, how you could spell *hell* or even *Shell Oil* on it when you entered the right numbers and looked at them upside down), mini-binoculars, Jew's harps, a pitch pipe, antique Iowa postcards. Unidentifiable crumbly bits, once erasers, or rubber bands perhaps? Food?

Drives from airports and train stations. The classical music station always on, the dad's quizzes: Okay, quick, name the composer. The dad knew the kid would most likely not know, but guesses would be made. Handel! Close, the dad would say.

Driving around his small hometown, pointing out sites he'd pointed out on every trip before: I've probably shown you the old mill, he'd say, exactly the same way, each time, passing the miniature mill by the train station. You know which one of those is your great-grandmother's house, right? Yes, the kid would say, even though there are two nearly alike (both small white clapboard) and the kid was never sure. We lived in that apartment on the square, above where the newsstand used to be, when I was born.

Do memories of photos count, if you can't remember the Kodak moment itself? This is a funny thing. The kid always claims to remember nothing from before the parents split, but of course stories get told, and in conjunction with the photographs (the dad reading her *Hop on Pop*, showing her a rose garden, the kid, in PJ's, on the dad's shoulders, the dad and the kid dyeing Easter eggs), well, it's just hard to know what's what. She has been told that early on, the mom was absent for long stretches (the grandmother was always happy to point these things out about her then daughter-in-law), that the dad taught her to read, put up giant flash cards with words on them around the house—REFRIGERATOR, TELEPHONE, CHAIR—has been told about the time when she was three and asked why there was an *S* missing from the Esso sign, about the time they had something flambé in a restaurant and she said I'm not scared, Daddy, are you? Is it enough that she remembers the dad telling her these stories, if not the actual events?

But what did they *talk* about? School? TV? Fuzzy. Circa 1972, she remembers him telling her about how he'd cracked the code on the expiration date on the Pop-Tarts box. She remembers his recipe for a sweet treat when you're out of everything else: bread with butter and sugar. They must have talked about writing, they wrote about writing, often, but whatever was said is in a cloud somewhere.

She remembers the dad opening a small cardboard box. Inside, tissue paper cradling fragile drips of molten lead. Telling her how he saved up bottle caps to make these, showing her how to melt them down and pour them into cold water to make interesting drips. How he, as a kid, had made coins out of molten lead, for the country he and his friends had started. How he showed her their manifesto, in a small green loose-leaf: maps, laws, accordances, amendments.

The dad taking the kid to the newsstand and buying her every single comic book she wanted, *Archie*, *Betty and Veronica*, *Richie Rich* on occasion. Sending her a subscription to *Barbie Talk*. But how she was jealous that when her half-sister was a kid, he kept a list of all the books she ever read. Sure, he might have done this for her too, if.

If this hadn't happened:

The young mom and dad met in small-town Iowa, fell in love? (who knows about that part, different versions have been reported), got married, got a kid, three years in the mom decided she needed to get away from the dad, be famous (plus it was the mid-'60s, she was no budding hippie or even budding feminist, but may still have been influenced by the times just as she claimed to have been influenced by the previous times, during which according to her she got married young because it was what you did), left kid with the dad, went to NY, got an apartment, came back in a couple years to get kid, told the dad don't call don't write (or something), kid didn't see the dad for a long while. This has all been explored in detail elsewhere, the mom parts. The mom parts are the dramatic parts, the no-way-really? parts, the I-can't-believe-the-kid's-not-more-fucked-up parts, the parts that felt urgent, when written. You are *lazy*, the mom said, often. You are lazy and *selfish* and (but?) I love you.

The kid has a question she's been asking for a while: Where is the story in the nonstory? Can the dad story be told without the conflict? It's not that there was zero conflict, only by comparison to the mom conflict. Is it even possible for mom conflict to be altogether separate from any dad conflict? Is it really true that that's what a story is, conflict? The kid recalls actually telling this to the dad, more than a few times, that a story wasn't a story without conflict. The dad wrote a novel once. A novella. It was a romance. All dialogue. Wasn't altogether bad, but had a couple of critical flaws, in her opinion: (1) It had sex. (Picture her reading this, the adult kid, not just sex but sex where the characters are forced to talk about what they're doing to each other, not just sex but sex written by her *dad*, as if suffering through endless talk about sex from her mom hadn't been plenty enough talk about sex for one kid's lifetime). (2) It had no conflict.

This story sucks. It's all over the place and the mom is creeping in again. Fuck her.

So the kid told the dad that his story had no conflict and the dad said he didn't like conflict, which she already knew to be true. He liked happy endings. He liked Disney movies. Someone always falls in the water in a Disney movie, he told her. You can count on it. In real life, the kid shared this nonconflict preference with her father, though she was perhaps less committed to avoiding it as he was. She thought she was, but it seemed to just "come up." The kid did some drinking, later, which can be an informal invitation to conflict.

This story sucks so bad it doesn't even know what tense it's in.

Whatever.

So but after the kid got to see the dad again after two years of nothing, mostly things were actually really great with her and the dad, except for the fucked-up things the mom—what if we tried calling her "the other parent"—had said about the dad that crept into her head sometimes (things that were by and large either untrue, dubious, or irrelevant to his skills as a parent), and later, for a time, became true-ish seeming, but really, were the same as the other parent's problems with everybody. It was all their fault. You may need some preventive therapy, sweetheart, to deal with your father issues.

Dad story. Get it together, writer.

So the kid went to Iowa for visits, hung out with the dad, got a stepfamily, a very nice, very mom-ish stepmom, same-age-ish siblings, it was fun, not like NY, they had like, lemonade stands and shit, and they laughed a lot at dinner, the dad and the siblings and the other mom were all funny, the kid was funny!, everyone was funny, Iowa was so super fun, and they did things together, as a family, they went camping together and played games all day and had running family jokes about big fat rats (not funny to you, right? and yet forty years later, to them, guess what, *still hilarious*) and went to drive-in movies and even made movies, like movie-movies, comedy movies, that the family all starred in and the dad directed and edited (with like, tape—the dad showed the kid how to do it) and then when we watched them in the family room (there was a *family* room, it had *beanbag* chairs, beanbag chairs! and shag carpeting! so good!) the other mom made popcorn in a big giant black tub, that's how much popcorn was needed, because there were so many of us having all this fun.

This story can't get its tense together *or* its person, now. Has it even got its *its* right? We don't know.

So this all went on for some years, Little League games, road trips, always in the summer, of course, or over Christmas or Easter break, those were the only times of year the kid was there, the rest of the time she was at home in NY, writing letters with the dad. Often, she wished there'd be a phone call or two, but this was a term the parents had psychically agreed upon. Too expensive, one said, not out loud, I don't want to hear that one's voice, said the other. Guess which one was which. Even travel arrangements were all sorted out by mail, over the course of any number of letters, months in advance. So, but it's good to have the letters, now that the dad is gone. Because the memory of the phone calls, the ones that hadn't happened, well, as has been implied, memory is weird. The kid can hear the dad's younger, better voice, if she tries hard, it was sort of a baritone, very smooth, but the crackly, fading voice is the one that comes up more often. She remembers the silent laughs from at the end, where his eyes would crinkle up like they always did, but little sound came out. Anyway, there weren't very many phone calls until maybe the '90s, so it's moot. There are letters that can be read, and what was said was what was said. And the letters are good. The dad said nice things to the kid, letter after letter, decade after decade, encouraging things, things that weren't confusing. And sent typewriters and reference books and TVs. The other parent thought the dad was trying to buy the kid's love but the kid thought the dad knew who the kid was and what would you have done if you were him?

So the kid grew up, went to college, got out of college, went to NY (where else would she go?), moved back home, it's NY, it's what everyone did, moved out a year later after it sucked enough, went to therapy, the usual story, the other parent fucked the kid up (the same-sex parent, typical), but due to the aforementioned particular methods utilized in this fucking up, for a period of time, the kid got this idea that it was the dad that fucked the kid up, at least partly. She had heard the other parent say so enough times that she began to believe it. That was dumb. This would get straightened out soon enough (e.g. she remembers a therapy session: Q: So how exactly are you selfish? A: ___. *Oh.* The therapy equivalent of the discovery of electricity or something). In the meantime, the dad being the dad, he was always patient and forgiving about it. More letters, always letters, even though the kid was now an adult, supposedly, and could have asked for—made—a phone call herself now and again—there must have been *some* phone calls but this seems fuzzy too—anyway, there were letters, in which the dad was funny and supportive and sent clippings of relevant things (articles about the Iowa Writers' Workshop, book reviews, pictures of pug dogs) and never said shit about the other parent and yet *lazy selfish I love you* were the things swimming around in her head for years and years (what do you *do* with those things together?) and then the kid finally thought to move away from NY, that had been someone else's choice, and the place where she went was a good bit closer to where the dad lived and she could and did visit more often, and not at legally dictated intervals. And this was good.

In these years, amends of a sort were made, though the dad indicated that amends were never needed, that's the kind of guy he was, and he visited her and she visited him and they played games and watched cheesy TV shows and went to the movies at the one movie theater in the square, and they went to the Old Threshers Reunion every year and looked at old threshers and antiques and he always bought her a little gewgaw or two she admired, which was so sweet, and this was all very good. Did the dad ever say an annoying declarative thing or two where the kid would just wish he'd end the sentence with *in my opinion*? Yes. This was a flaw of the dad—he was very smart and very knowledgeable about many things and he knew this about himself and sometimes it carried over into his opinions, and sometimes, possibly most times, he was even intending this rhetoric to be funny, the kid was sure, but anyway this was his flaw that sometimes bugged her. Did she ever wish the dad would stand up for himself, like the time he got the home movies put on video? Yes? This was a great thing, ostensibly, but some stuff got edited out, and the dad had been upset but hadn't wanted to bother anyone about it, what was done was done. That had seemed like a big deal to her, losing whatever that footage was, though the kid didn't even know what was lost. Something important having to do with her childhood. And then also he got cancer and shit and then Parkinson's, but failed to ask some obvious-seeming questions, because he didn't want to bother the doctors. And then what's a kid supposed to do, berate her ailing dad about it? It was useless to explain that this constituted a good part of the doctor's job, of the services the dad was paying him for, being bothered. Wasn't the father, so smart, smart enough to know this? On the other hand, had asking questions of doctors helped her other parent not die? Not so much.

The point is, he was a person, right, no one is perfect, and the kid doesn't want you to think that this is some story where there's this idealized, perfect parent thing. She's mostly just trying to not forget things. Anyway, there were a lot of good years, letters in the mail became emails (the dad's idea!). The kid remembers this very well, how she thought, oh, the internet, nobody really uses that, and how frustrating her early attempts to get service were, and how the dad did his best to help her figure it out (he'd been an electronics engineer in the navy, always loved technology, had a computer in the house back in the '70s he'd been so excited about: It's hooked up to the university! Look what you can do! Punch cards with Christmas trees, banners on continuous paper, with dot-matrix birthday greetings!). Her protests: But haven't letters always been so great? His counterpoints: Email would be like instant letters. Some trial and error later, emails became daily, and phone calls finally went into the mix as well. How he would leave long phone messages that always ended with *Love, Dad*.

You may need some preventive therapy. Father issues. Lazy.

Lazy lingering there in the kid's head, long after the mom was gone, even though she'd by this time written four books and done a bunch of other pretty good shit too. (Should she have written five, six, twenty? Earned more per book? What are the acceptable numbers for crossing the lazy-to-productive divide?)

For fuck's sake already. The mom has had her stories. This is not her story.

End with the dad! End with the dad!

The dad, returning from the daughter's back porch to report on the rap music coming from the alley. Something about motherfucking hos, he said.

The dad, at a bookstore, to a favorite author of the daughter's. My daughter is a published writer too!

The dad, in his office. I just wanted to say how proud I am of you.

Father issues. Seriously? He's not the one who haunts her dreams.

The dad's reception of the future son-in-law. I would like your permission to marry your daughter. Hm, I've never been asked this before. What do I do? You say yes, Dad! Oh, okay, well then yes! The dad and the husband at the kitchen table. These were my father's tools. These were my wooden soldiers. These were the wood block prints I made in high school. These are my ten thousand Jew's harps. These are my art books, maybe you'd like to have some of them. The dad and the husband. The dad and the husband. They both carry hankies.

The time the dad picked her up at the train and took her suitcase, as usual. There hadn't been a struggle so much as just a moment, one in which the kid noticed that her dad was about to be old. The time the dad drove up on the curb, the time he scraped her car with the riding mower even though he had a wide berth. The dad had never been a good driver, predicted his own death by lollygagging at the wheel. That wasn't how it went down; he stopped driving not too long after these incidents.

The progress of the illness: slow, after this, but predictable. Wobbling, walker, wheelchair, hospital-bed-lifter-into contraption, so many pills and timers for pills, assorted cognitive issues. A different story.

Holidays during this time, adult kids and grandkids and grandcats and granddogs, watching movies of us watching movies, making the same comments on the original movies, Dad in his wheelchair, his voice too weak to speak, yet wiping tears of laughter with his hanky. The herky-jerky, smiling face via Skype when he couldn't talk so well. She remembers now, a conversation about a favorite bit from *Infinite Jest*, about the failure of video phones. How the dad laughed when she read it to him. How he wondered when his daughter started reading such highfalutin' stuff (his use of words like *highfalutin'* purposeful; he liked to portray himself as folksy which was maybe one part of him, even though he'd grown up privileged, faux-folksiness called into question when he would point out, for example, that the proper pronunciation of *creek* was *crick* and so forth).

A last little shaky wave good-bye. Love you, Dad, always.

Acknowledgments

Grateful acknowledgment to following publications for including versions of the following stories: *The Huffington Post* ("Everywhere, Now"), *Guernica* ("The Genius Meetings," "Notes for a Dad Story"), *The Coachella Review* ("Star Babies"), *Rookie* ("Roosters"), *Make* ("Here Everything's Better"), *Bat City Review* ("Some Concerns," original title "Fear of a Terrible Wife"), *Fifty-Two Stories* anthology ("Looking," original title "I Like Looking at Pictures of Gwen Stefani"), *Swink* ("All the Wigs of the World"), *Fairy Tale Review* ("Mr. and Mrs. P Are Married"), *DimeStories* ("Best Friends Seriously Forever"), *Chicago Quarterly Review* ("Justin Bieber's Hair in a Box"), *The Lifted Brow* ("Notes for an Important American Story"), *Who Can Save Us Now?* anthology ("Heroes," original title "Nate Pinckney Alderson, Superhero"), *The Collagist* ("Turf"), *Fields* ("Video"), *Hobart* ("Wind"), *Commentary* ("We Collect Things")

With so much gratitude to Nina Solomon for being my first reader (and personal cheerleader), always, and to Kirk Walsh,

Duncan Murrell, Jamie Quatro, and Roy Kesey for their help in getting these stories where they needed to go. Your notes have been invaluable and you're just dear people.

Alice Tasman, there aren't enough words to say how glad I am to know you, and thanks as well to everyone at JVNLA for their continued hard work on my behalf. Dan Smetanka, as a longtime fan of you the editor and you the person, I'm super thrilled that we've taken our relationship to the next level (wink emoji); Lucille has been necessary but merciful to this work, and I am grateful. To my UCR friend-leagues, I just adore all of you, and your handholding is not the least of what helps me carry on with this whole writing thing.

I wrote early versions of some of these stories a good long while ago now, and as such, I beg forgiveness in advance if you read them and gave me notes and I forgot. Consider this me signing off on whatever you have to do in the way of subtweets.

And to Ben, my favorite everything.

Author photograph by Joshua Brown Photography

About the Author

Elizabeth Crane is the author of the novels *The History of Great Things* and *We Only Know So Much* and three collections of short stories. Her stories have been featured on NPR's *Selected Shorts*. She is a recipient of the Chicago Public Library 21st Century Award, and her work has been adapted for the stage by Chicago's Steppenwolf Theatre Company. She currently lives in Newburgh, New York. Please visit www.elizabethcrane.com to learn more.